Daniel Malden

This is, to all intents and purposes, a true story.
However, on occasions, when the author has been
forced to decide between historical accuracy and
dramatic effect, history has usually come off worse.
Nevertheless, this is at least a possible story, and
one that Daniel Malden and his contemporaries
might well have recognised, and even laid claim to.

The story of
Daniel Malden

PIP WRIGHT

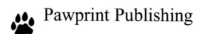 Pawprint Publishing

ISBN 978-0-9548298-5-8

Published by **Pawprint Publishing**
14, Polstead Close, Stowmarket, Suffolk   IP14 2PJ

Acknowledgements

are due to Clare Barker, who was able to translate something I couldn't.
Thanks are also due to the staff at the Suffolk Record Offices at Ipswich, Bury
St. Edmunds and Lowestoft, the Family History Centre at Norwich, the
Library of the National Maritime Museum, The Horseracing Museum at
Newmarket, Cambridge University Library, The Bodleian Library, The
London Metropolitan Archive and the National Portrait Gallery

Front cover design by Daniel Wright

Printed by **Polstead Press**, 5 Stowupland Road.,
Stowmarket, Suffolk IP14 5AG

for Julie

Daniel Malden

Chapter 1
The words of Daniel Malden Senior ~ 1712

It's an odd kind of fame that is based on notoriety. At his death, my son Daniel was probably the most famous man in the nation. His story had been repeated in the papers and on the lips of people of all levels of society. Carriers took tales of Dan Malden from city to town to village. Reports of his eventual demise reached Philadelphia and New York. People read descriptions of his life and death as though they were a fiction. For a brief moment in time, the name of Daniel Malden was spoken of in the streets and was on the minds of everyone. But it will soon be all forgotten; you can be sure of that.

I remember the day he was born, above a joiner's shop in Ipswich in the year 1712: tiny, perfect, a boy with his whole life before him. Not that I knew much about it. Birthing was women's work and it was the women that saw to it. I took myself off, leaving the work I knew I should be doing - the work that judging by past experience I might never be paid for. Being a craftsman can be a thankless task. You lay out your own money on the materials you need, you put a lifetime's learning into your craft and you use such skills as you possess to fashion an article of rare beauty. Then you spend three months wrangling over the bill. No, though there was work to be done, it would wait. Without thought of where I was heading, I found my feet taking me down by the dock.

It was dull and cool, but at least the rain had eased. A number of ships lay at anchor, for the most part beached high and dry on the mud. Just a few were anchored in the stream. Ipswich was a poor excuse for a port then. Silt had gathered, so the larger ships came no more. The few that did had to wait until the tide was on the full in order to dock. The winter past, the anchorages had cleared and trade had dropped, though no-one seemed to care any more. Portmen enjoyed the rights and benefits of their position. Few considered their responsibilities. I could see that and I was, to all intents and purposes, an outsider.

Across the river from where I stood that day were the shipbuilding yards with all the evidence of their associated trades - the repairers, caulkers, sailstitchers, ropemakers. A smell of malting and tar lay sweet on the air. That was where I had come to find much of my work at the time. Skilled joiners were rare in the boatyards then; there was less call for them. Once, great naval vessels had been built in our yards, but all that trade had gone to London and we were building colliers for Newcastle and Gateshead instead. The finishing work was my responsibility. Most days I worked at home, crafting the details that still made Ipswich boats carry the respect of the nation. Other places would use any half-apprenticed carpenter to do what I did, with the inevitable results.

That was one day I couldn't work. I told myself it was too cold to grasp the tools; and with it being Mary's time, I was best away from the place. There were things I could have done afloat, on the bridge of a hull that had been floated the week before. But I couldn't put my mind to it, and it would have meant finding a ferryman to carry me over - so many excuses! In the end, I just walked in circles, returning every little while to the house in the hope of some sign of an end to it. It was taking hours. I was young and impatient.

By the water's edge, a big black cormorant was struggling to deal with an eel it had caught. The fish must have been as long as the bird was tall, but it was determined to swallow the thing whole. Once or twice the eel slithered from the bird's grasp and attempted to wriggle back to the safety of the water. Each time, the cormorant pulled it away onto the mud and tried to work the eel's head into its open mouth. But all this effort had not gone unnoticed, and a pair of gulls set about the cormorant in an attempt to help themselves to an easy meal. Beak firmly clamped on the writhing fish, the cormorant tried to fly off, but the weight of the fish and the mobbing by the gulls was too much, and it found itself airborne minus its meal. Even then the gulls could not agree to share what they had won and as they bickered and squabbled over their prize, the eel was away and gone, safe in the depths of the harbour to await the outgoing tide.

To kill time, I stopped for a jug in the Black Horse. That led to another and still more, so that by the time I got home, I'd practically forgotten why I'd gone out in the first place. I soon sobered up when I saw my son. My boy Daniel. He would have my name and maybe, in time, my skills. Mary was tired and weak, but she was made from strong stock - she would survive. I went out back to find coals for a fire. Both mother and baby had to be kept warm. I had a store ready and waiting. From time to time, colliers were sent to Ipswich for a refit. If you were lucky, you could find a stone or two of coal below decks. It was precious - too precious to use, except at times like this.

Seeing I was back, old Nancy, the midwife, made her exit. Mother and child seemed well and she had seen enough births to recognise that her job was over for the time being. And at least Mary's mother was close at hand to play her part.

It was strange; for the first time since I had come to Ipswich, I felt that I belonged. In a few short months I had become both a husband and a father. Somehow that puts a different light on things. As I may have hinted, our marriage had been something of a hurried affair. Mind you, I know others that cut it finer. One couple at their wedding, I heard, had a midwife waiting in the church porch just in case her services should be required sooner than those of the parson.

I'd only moved to Ipswich for Mary's sake. It was her town, her parish, and I'd had my doubts about settling there, but it was proving the kind of place where people of modest means could make a living. The gentry and nobility may not have been attracted there, and the docks had certainly declined, but few beggars roamed the streets and there was a moderate air of prosperity about the place. At least, I hoped, it would prove an end to my wanderings.

My family had come from a small village near Bury St. Edmunds. Like most, I was of labouring stock. But increased enclosure meant the day of the smallholder was gone. My parents had pleaded with the parish to find me an apprenticeship. I hadn't wanted it, as I knew it would mean leaving home, and probably the area I knew. In the end I was placed with a joiner in Newmarket... seven years spent learning everything that man knew, which wasn't enough, and it would be at least another five before I could call myself a craftsman.

It was about then that I first met Mary Brasier. Her father worked with horses and had been responsible for training a number that had achieved success at Ipswich Races. Attracted by the Newmarket prize money, the owners he represented wanted him to run their horses there. At the time, I was drawn to the sport. I would place wagers for certain gentlemen who didn't wish their wives or fathers or business partners to know they liked to bet.

In the spring of 1710, Mary had come with her father, which was when we first met. Rightaway, we knew we were right for one another. After that, she would return at any opportunity. I moved to Ipswich the following year just to be nearer to her. That was when I found my niche, fitting out boats after the shipbuilders had finished. It wasn't hard to find a house to rent with a downstairs room that would serve as a workshop. I ended up renting a property not far from Mary's home, and began to generate work and a reputation.

The summer of 1711, we both went with her father to run horses at Newmarket. That was a joyous time. We dressed as finely as our purses would allow and mingled with the titled and the wealthy; which was not always one and the same thing. The finest thoroughbreds were raced there, bred from champions, some from Italy and Arabia. Though these were still early days, and it was before the Jockey Club began meeting at Vernon's Coffee House, fashion reigned supreme and the colour and excitement was second to none. Though we knew we didn't really belong in this world, it was easy to feel free and abandoned and forget about our lives back in Ipswich. On Newmarket Heath, at the end of the July meeting, my son was conceived, though it would be a few months before I would know anything about it.

Give her her due, Mary didn't want me to feel trapped; she didn't want me to feel I *had* to marry her. But I never felt that way. I was pleased as punch when I knew I was going to be a father. Marrying Mary was all I ever wanted, and a son just put the topping on the cake. Somehow I knew all along it would be a boy. I could imagine all the things I wanted him to be - he would know from an early age about tools and their use. I could see he was schooled. I could read a little; write less. I was determined to ensure his start in life would be better than mine. Ipswich may not have been the perfect place to live, but it had schools and there was no need for children to grow up ignorant or illiterate.

Maybe he would see the world. I watched ships come and go daily. Most commuted between East coast ports, but others were bound for more exotic climes. Well-travelled tars would throng to the quayside taverns, weaving tales of mermaids and sea-serpents, whales and dark-skinned maidens. Perhaps he would ride horses, winning races for Mary's father and his clients. Yes, I told myself, there were so many things he would do that his father could only dream of.

We saw a lot of Mary's family in those early days. A number dwelt nearby, but even those who lived in Essex made the effort to visit us quite regularly. They were a close family.

It took a bit longer for my parents to make the journey, first to Bury, then by coach to Ipswich. I was so glad to see them. The

Brasier clan were wearing me out. We had made our house comfortable and inviting; too much so maybe.

I remember one particular relation, one of many we entertained at the time. He had a pretty wife and a daughter. The child was about five years old and delightful to behold, but there was something about her that just didn't seem right. Behind that angelic face was a deceitful and scheming little mind - a dreadful thing to say about a child, I know, but true enough. Strangely her name was the same as my wife's had been before we had married - Mary Brasier. She was fascinated by the tools in my workshop; especially the sharpest blades. I took care to see she did not harm herself. Her parents seemed unconcerned.

My son Daniel was in his cot. As the adults chatted, having first made a fuss of the baby, I am sure I caught sight of that monstrous child trying to smother him. Of course she swore she was extricating the baby from his bedclothes, which had become tangled. And of course her parents said what a little heroine she was for noticing such a thing. I knew differently and remained vigilant for the rest of the visit, which was, thankfully, short. After they left, I noticed one of my sharpest chisels was missing. I never knew for certain where it had gone, but I had my suspicions.

Twenty-five years later, when she was transported to Virginia, Mary Brasier got her just desserts. Oh that it had been five years earlier.

When my parents finally came to see their grandson, it was something of a shock to me. My father had changed so much. Time had not favoured him. My mother seemed little different. Her aging had come early. Now it was his turn. It was clear why. The work was harder and the rewards less. But they were so excited to see and hold their first grandchild. And I had so much to show them. My parents had rarely strayed from the village in which they had both been born. A trip to Bury Fair was for them the journey of a lifetime. Now they were in Ipswich, a town of over twelve thousand people. There were so many things to see... the docks, the Assembly Rooms, the ancient walls and gates, the street entertainers, the market stalls: all the activity and the bustle of a large town.

Unlike my boy Daniel, I was not destined to travel. But I can imagine, as I later travelled to London to see my son, the impression Ipswich must have made on *my* father. I would only see him once more after that, but I am so glad I was able to take his breath away, before the Lord did, permanently.

Two days later, we all went to see them off, Mary, Daniel and I. As the coach pulled away from the Coach and Horses, we waved and called out, "Come again, soon!" …the way you do.

"I like your dad," Mary said as we walked back across town. "He's a real gen'leman."

By that time, it was high summer, and hot and dusty. We were cheerful enough but as I recall, we were about to embark on the worst difference of opinion we ever had. It was all about our son's baptism. Though I had been raised to attend the parish church and we had married at St Matthews, of late I had been drawn to a new independent church in the town. There, they were of a mind to postpone baptising infants until such time as they could come to God of their own free will. Mary did not share my views and there was no shaking either of us over this matter.

"And what if he dies?" she cried, "He will go to his God unforgiven."

"He is a child," I tried to explain. "What is there to forgive?"

"Think of our families; they will not understand." She was trying a different argument. But I was having none of it.

"I can't change the way I believe just to satisfy our parents."

"Then change it to satisfy me." She pleaded, but it did no good. It only made things worse when we widened the debate and elders from both churches became involved. In the end an uneasy settlement came about whereby it was agreed I would be responsible for the religious wellbeing of my firstborn son and Mary would be free to take any other children we might produce to St. Matthews for infant baptism. That was how it came to be that our three daughters, Mary, Sarah and Elizabeth and even our other boy, John, were christened within sight of our house. Daniel, I admit to my regret, never was a part of any church. By the time he was of an age to decide such things for himself, he had already embarked on an opposite path.

The night after Dan was born, we laid down beside one another, Mary and I. We went to sleep, hand clutching hand, and never felt so close. There were those in both of our churches who said it was a sin for a man to lay beside his wife after childbirth until she had been churched; before she had been cleansed. But you can do no better than what feels right, and nothing felt more right than our togetherness did then, and our mutual satisfaction in a job well done.

It was shortly after that, two things happened to cause concern in out lives. Early that autumn Mary became quite sick. Others in the parish had died of an odd and uncommon fever. She was still feeding the child, but became less able to and it was as if the disease was to threaten both of them. Fortunately, it became possible to wean the baby from his mother. Which just left Mary. At that time, Doctor Beeston had a physick garden in the town where it was rumoured he grew such herbs as could cure all malcontents of the body and mind. My problem was I had worked most of the summer for one boatbuilder and had yet to see any payment. Elixirs do not come cheap. Nevertheless, I borrowed such money as was necessary to purchase a remedy. Describing Mary's symptoms, I went with the doctor to his garden. It was a truly remarkable place. On the bank of the river and with a southerly aspect, the flowers growing there would have graced any grand mansion. I do not know the names of all that he gathered for Mary's treatment. Suffice it to say, I recognised borage and sorrel and hellebore, but there were others that were foreign to me and have encountered them neither before nor since. I am ever grateful to that man, for though it placed me in a situation of debt, from the next day, when I prepared the herbs as instructed, Mary began to recover. However, my hopes of rapidly returning the money lent to me were dashed when the shipbuilder absconded, leaving my debt greatly increased. Oh, those were low times! In her sickness, I tried to keep this from Mary, but she could sense, in the way a true wife can, that something was very wrong and I had to confess I was in danger of being unable to meet the demands of my creditors. As I said, two matters arose at that time. It was the second that would solve my problem, though I still find it hard to believe the risk I was prepared to undertake.

About a week after Mary had risen from her sick-bed, I was hard at work. It was the only way I knew to handle my predicament. Mary was now fit to look after the child again and long hours of toil lay ahead of me.

"Master Malden?"

I heard the voice, but I did not look up, as I was involved in a fine piece of work. I am not by trade a wood-carver, but from time to time, it was necessary to apply a little carving to embellish a piece of my work. It took all my concentration to get it right, so I did not look up.

"If you'll be Master Malden as I suspect you are, my colleagues might be after offering you some business."

I still did not look up. I so often received offers of work that amounted to nothing, it seemed more appropriate to finish what I was doing. I just acknowledged his words with no apparent enthusiasm.

"If you speak to my wife, she will acquaint you with my terms."

"I don't think you understand, Master Malden. We dictate our own terms, but at least we offer an advance, which I am sure is more than most of your customers do."

If anything was guaranteed to grab my attention, an offer of payment in advance was it. Without wanting to seem too eager,

I put down my chisel and looked upon the face of the speaker for the first time. He was a tall, thick-set man, about five feet nine in height and wearing a wig beset with a tall hat, not unlike those worn by naval officers. For all that, his jacket was faded and patched and he gave the appearance of one who spent his life on the road... or at sea. The more I thought about it, I began to worry. I was never paid in advance for my joinery, so what... just what was I expected to do?

"You have a cellar here? It is dry?" It did not seem as if he expected an answer. Presumably he had made his enquiries. Still, I answered.

"Yes, it is dry in all but the most extreme conditions. I use it to store wood and provisions."

"You could empty it?" The voice was more insistent now.

"I could, but to what purpose?"

"My colleagues would like to use it to store some of the products they are trading in."

In a flash, I could see what I was being asked to do. There were tales of what was known as the Cat-House on the banks of the Orwell where the owner would stand a stuffed cat in his window to let the local smugglers know when a run was imminent. We all knew the extent to which the coast and the creeks were landing points for all the most highly taxed commodities. We also knew that few of the real smugglers ended up being caught. No, it was the poor fools who harboured the men or their booty who ended up in gaol or dangling at the end of a rope. The way the authorities worded it, depriving His Majesty of his revenue was almost a treasonable act. My first reaction was to send the man packing. But he was made of sterner stuff than that and I was in severe financial difficulties. In the end I listened to what he had to say and was almost convinced. Revenue men were thin on the ground in the county. The network of smugglers and distributors was vast. There was little chance of any one cache being found. It would not remain there long. I could even earn more by making a few deliveries around the town. As a local tradesman, I would not be likely to fall under suspicion. Oh yes, it all sounded so easy. And I could pay off my debts immediately. So like a fool, I fell in with them. But, if I thought I could keep it from Mary, I had another think coming.

"Why have you moved all that wood out of the cellar?" she asked.

"Winter's coming on - it might flood."

"It might have flooded last winter but you didn't move it then."

"I want the wood close at hand. I'm going to be using it soon."

"What - all of it?"

"There's a few boxes I want to put down in the cellar for the moment."

"Boxes of what?"

"Just boxes - you know, this and that."

"Would this have anything to do with the man with the ring?"

I hadn't even noticed a ring.

"You know what kind of men wear rings like that?" Mary asked.

She didn't wait for my reply. "Your fine gentleman had a coffin-ring on his finger, and I may be a simple Suffolk gal, but my daddy used to tell me 'bout things like that."

How could I not have noticed it. It was legendary. They said that the smugglers all wore a ring fashioned from coffin furniture that was supposed to defend them against the dragoons and those that sought to protect the miles of North Sea coast from the likes of them.

Funnily enough, Mary didn't seem too concerned and knew much more about the whole business than I did. It was still a mighty risk and I was far from happy about it. In the end, little Dan was the perfect cover for me. I made a small cart that the baby could ride in and under the pretext of visiting my customers, I visited customers of a different sort, with bottles and bundles

17

packed under the sleeping child. He liked the movement of the cart, and packets of Bohea tea made a comfortable mattress.

The goods came soon after I had cleared the cellar and I was even encouraged to put back some of the wood to conceal the barrels and chests and bundles stored there. Under cover of darkness, men brought tea and brandy, coffee and gin, fabrics and even human hair for the making of the finest wigs. It had come from favourite landing points like Levington and Bawdsey, Orford and Misner Haven, brought in carts and on the backs of teams of ponies. They reckoned half of Ipswich drank tea that had lodged in my cellar and a good portion of the spirits served in the taverns arrived by the same route. My new masters knew I was basically an honest man, you see. Others watered down the gin and kept some of the best for themselves. They would shred oak leaves to replace the tobacco they had filched; sloe leaves were mixed with tea to make it go further. Wig-powder would be corrupted with chalk or flour. There were hundreds of ways to cheat both your customers and your suppliers. Tea that looked too pale because half of it wasn't tea at all could be coloured. I heard of someone that used copper and ended up poisoning the poor souls that drank the stuff. To my credit, I never played any of these tricks. I just turned a blind eye to the way my premises was being used and helped move the stuff out as fast as I possibly could. Which was fine, until the excise men came calling.

I was woken early one morning the following summer by a hammering on the door. A man I did not recognise introduced himself as Mr. Newby. He was a preventative officer and had a warrant to search my home. He had brought with him one soldier in case I put up any resistance. Of course that was not my way. I was already resigned to a gaol sentence or at the worst, transportation to America. Ours was not a large house and it soon became clear that the only possible hiding place was down below. Finding a number of suspicious kegs and bundles wrapped in waxed paper, Mary and I were placed under house arrest and the young dragoon left to guard both the two of us and the store of contraband. Fortunately, the officer had received notice of a larger hoard at Woodbridge and had arranged to meet up with others to go in pursuit of the smugglers and their illicit goods. He was likely to be some time.

I felt cold and helpless. Luckily Mary took matters in hand. She was by this time big with child again. She sat beside the young man and started to talk to him in a friendly voice as if she had known him all her life.

"You realise," she began, "we know nothing of what is down in the cellar. My husband is a joiner; he works long hours. He has no time for searching cellars. We are away from the house a lot; at the docks or at my mother's. It would be very easy for people to put things there when we were out."

"Save your breath," I thought. "It will not be he who judges us… and condemns us."

"I'm sorry ma'am," said the young soldier, "but if that is what we think it is, then you will be telling this to the court."

Exactly!

"Perhaps," Mary suggested sweetly, "we should see just what is down there. After all, if it is nothing, then we are all wasting our time."

That made sense to the young man, even if it didn't to me. I knew only too well what was in those barrels: several hundred ankers of Geneva. I had had a sip myself. But it was not just a sip Mary offered the young soldier; more like a tankard full. And that was just from the first barrel. After that there were all the rest to try. By the time, the officer returned half a day later, he found the cellar empty except for one snoring soldier. The evidence gone and in danger of being regarded as a laughing stock, the officer left in high dudgeon, probably intending to take his anger out on his young accomplice, when he sobered up.

Mary and I knew just how lucky we'd been. It was a salutary lesson to us not to place ourselves in such a position again. We were worried it might prove difficult to free ourselves from the employ of the smugglers, but we needn't have feared.

As far as the smugglers were concerned, our house was no longer a safe haven. For ourselves, though the money had been useful, we were not sorry to know our role in this affair had come to an end. We could get back on with the rest of our lives, with a growing trade, one baby already and another on the way. Life was good.

Chapter 2
The words of Mary Malden ~ 1721 & 1723

"Dan!" I called as loudly as I could. It was no use; he was nowhere to be found. He never was when he was needed. And what was worse, I could be sure he was up to no good with those friends of his. *'The Orwell Urchins'* they called them: nimble-toed and light-fingered lot they were. He wouldn't listen to a word I said; his father neither. I've given birth to four children to date, and which was the one who never slept at night as a baby? Which was the one who wouldn't do a thing he was told from the outset? Which, of course, was the one his father idolised and would hear no criticism of his precious firstborn?

And just for the record, which was the one who was not taken to St. Matthews and given a douse of Holy Water by way of a baptism? 'He would come to God in his own time'... Fine chance of that!

"Dan!" It was still no good. Even if he were within hearing, he'd be bound to do the opposite of what his parents wanted. What a child! Was a mother ever so slighted? Somehow I knew it would not be long before others would call his name: others whose calls could not be so easily ignored. We did our best; nobody could suggest we didn't. His father would have taught him his trade, except he wouldn't stay around long enough to learn anything.

We intended he would have an education - the opportunity was there, but he would not apply himself; turned his back on every chance of improvement. If I took him to school, he would run away. He saw little purpose in reading and writing, though he was quick enough when he wanted to be.

It seems a terrible thing to say, but he appeared destined from an early age to err on the side of evil. It seems only weeks ago when the real disappointment came. In spite of all his contrariness, he had picked up enough of the basics of reading to be considered for the Greycoat School. We are so lucky in Ipswich; charitable foundations exist to see our children receive an education. Little Mary attends the Bluecoat School close by and she is promised a placement in service at the end of it. If Dan had been of a mind, he could have seen himself apprenticed in a year or two... but then came that terrible interview.

We both went, me carrying John in my arms and Daniel holding Sarah's hand. An impressive place it was; not like the parish school, noisy and crowded and stinking of poverty. No, it was quiet and orderly; the boys in their uniforms, seeming so studious. I should have known it was no place for Dan.

"Come in, Mr. and Mrs. Malden," the Supervisor said.

He looked grave and I'm sure we both looked uncomfortable.

"We were of a mind to take your son in the hope we could make something of him. As you know, our boys have a fine reputation. The education they gain here is such that they are much in demand as apprentices, and the foundation is only too pleased to pay for the right placement, providing the boys play their part."

"I'm sure..." began my husband.

"Playing their part means attending regularly, respecting their teachers and not abusing the opportunities offered to them."

We knew then that it was worse than we had expected. Indeed it was. The register of admissions sat open. It was the practice of the school to enter the boys' names on their departure. Most were placed with a trade. Occasionally, they failed to reach expectations and were expelled. I feared this would be the case with Dan, but in many ways it was worse.

"We cannot keep your son here any longer," the Supervisor continued. "Most of the time he is not here at all. He has been observed in unsuitable company conducting himself in an unseemly manner in the uniform of this school."

At that, he closed the book and my spirits rose - briefly.

"Now I learn he has not even been baptised. I took it for

granted as your other children's names are in the baptismal register of St. Matthews, Daniel's must be somewhere else. But he informs me in the most intrepid manner that he has no fear of God as - and I use his words here - God has so far failed to get his clutches on him."

That wretched business again!

"As you realise, this is a Christian foundation, and though our present parliament seems intent on recognising all kinds of ungodly organisations, the Greycoat School will remain a Christian foundation - Christian in attitude, Christian in act." He paused to draw breath. "I am not entering your son's name in this register as it is clear he should never have been admitted to this school in the first place. He is not being expelled, merely esponged from the record."

I sobbed - what more could I do. Little Sarah let go of her father's hand and came to comfort me. She gave the tall man a look of contempt - as much a look of contempt as it is possible for a four year-old to give.

The man's voice softened. "Of course, I know one rotten apple in an orchard does not corrupt the whole crop. Other children in your family will receive fair consideration should you want to educate them here (and giving Sarah a smile) or at our sister school. I looked at baby John lying so peaceful in my lap. At least his life need not be blighted by his brother's actions. And you know, for a moment I felt almost glad.

Dan didn't reappear until much later. He breezed in as though nothing had happened and none of it mattered. I was angry and of half a mind to give him no supper, but he had obviously found food (and ale), who knows where. That was the trouble; you could not find a way to punish him. I only saw his father beat him once, and it certainly pained him more sorely than the boy, who punished us both by disappearing for three days. We tried talking to him. We tried asking others to talk to him. But all to no avail. Then my father made a suggestion, one that we had not tried before.

"The lad is small. He is trying to make up for his lack of size with brashness and bravado. He needs experience of a world where his slightness of stature is a positive advantage."

Of course he meant working with horses. I don't know why we'd not considered it before. At the suggestion, Dan seemed quite keen, and to my surprise would rise early on the coldest of mornings to work with my father on the gallops above the foreshore. He was small, but tough and wiry and could cope with the strongest stallions. Though too young to ride races as a jockey, he was learning all the while about handling and care of horses. Someone gave him a jockey's cap, an old green one. He wore it night and day and it stayed with him long after he had abandoned the sport in favour of other things.

Racing drew a lot of money then, just as it does now. Prize money at courses like Ipswich, Newmarket and Beccles could run to hundreds of guineas. Wagers were placed for thousands. There were always going to be those unscrupulous people who would seek to find ways of influencing results by bribery or administering substances to either horse or rider. It was at one such event that trouble arose.

As I recall, it was August 1723. It was the week of the King's Plate at Bury, to be run on the Race Ground on the heath just outside the town. The Angel Hill was packed. All manner of diversions had been arranged. There were mains of cocks to fight at the Dog and Partridge, and entertainments for the ladies around the town. The latest comedy was showing at the Shire Hall. It was 'The Fond Husband' or 'The Widow's Revenge' or something like that. The most fashionable people were attracted to the town. But all classes of society were there. Tents and booths sprang up overnight on the heath. You could buy trinkets and toys, walnuts and pears and of course, horses. The Gipsy traders were there in abundance, aiming to double their money by staging prize-fights and side-shows.

There were curiosities too - the famous rat-killer, Mr Tom Wauff was there, telling of how he had once rid one house of over 1500 rats. There were freak shows and exhibitions of strength and courage; plenty to see if you had the money to spend, which, of course, I didn't. I went with my father and Dan. John was still only two, so he came with us, but the two girls stayed behind with their father, in spite of their moans and groans.

We arrived to find all of the owners and their representatives gathered around the Angel Hotel, the centre of town Tavern where registration was being carried out. You had to present your horses with certificates proving their age. There were also the fees to be paid. Jockeys in their owners' colours were present. Some of the younger gentlemen preferred to ride their own horses, but many couldn't make the ten stone weight and, rather than disadvantage their horse over a demanding four mile course, would employ a professional jockey. By this time, this was what Dan had set his heart upon.

We would not be involved in the major event, with its hundred-guinea prize. That was far too grand for the likes of us. That would be contested by the Dukes of Somerset and Devonshire. They owned real race horses, of Arabian stock, not hunters like those my father handled. Our horses might not have had the turn of foot, but they had strength and stamina and heart. They would stay the course and put in as strong a finish as many a rich man's mount.

We had brought three horses, two bay mares and a grey gelding. The race that particularly interested my father and his employers carried a thirty-guinea prize. It was for horses that had not won prize money of more than that in total before. There would be a series of heats, the prize being awarded to the first horse to win two of them. These would be run in just one day, so it favoured the strong. Only if one horse won a heat by a vast distance would a second heat not be required. Between the heats, horses would be watered, wiped down and kept warm. We knew we had a good chance and were feeling high on excitement.

It must have been then that Dan wandered off, and by the time we had registered the horses and found him again, he had made company with two others. They were introduced to us as Joseph Rose and Will Saunders. They spoke with the rough voices of Southern Essex or East London. I was not impressed, especially with Rose. He was about twenty-five and gave the impression he was permanently scheming. Saunders was younger, not much more than a lad but, from the way he spoke, was well acquainted with the horse fraternity. He had dark skin and a curl to his hair. He could have passed for a gipsy boy, and maybe that was his origin. He seemed bright enough but he was clearly under the spell of Joseph Rose, and that was one man I did not trust from the outset.

"Now the registration's done, I'm going with Will and Joe up to the heath," said Daniel.

He didn't ask. He announced. I knew there was money in his pocket. My father had paid him and he had kept it for this holiday. I could hardly object. There was not much to do other than set up camp on the heath and see the horses were comfortable. He would find us when his money ran out. An eleven year-old boy wanted a bit of freedom. I just wished he were in better company. I flashed a glance at Joseph Rose that said, "Look after him." He grinned back a smirk that inspired no confidence. No confidence at all!

Later that day, we received a visit.

"Good day to you sir." I curtsied, unsure how to behave. We had barely set up camp before the owner of the best of our horses (one of the bay mares) arrived to check all was well. As I recall, his name was Mr. Butler. I can see him now. So grand he looked, but he took trouble to put us at our ease. And he made such a fuss of little Johnny.

"And what is the name of this young lass?" he asked.

John had long blonde curls and was dressed in his sisters' best hand-me-downs. I mumbled that 'she' was a 'he' and he smiled and said simply, "Ah, a young jockey to be."

Dan was still missing and, to be honest, I wasn't sorry. He could prove unpredictable, and I didn't want to have to make excuses for him. The young man who was to ride the mare was also in attendance. He wore the owner's colours, blue and white, but not the actual silks he would ride in.

The mare looked in perfect condition and we all had high hopes of success. Bred in the vale of York, she had won just two purses of ten guineas, but now was ready to race for a larger prize. "I'll confess I've not seen a finer beast at this meet," Mr. Butler said to my father. Then he turned to me and to John. "...and if you have a guinea or two to spare, it might be well placed on our mare to win."

He continued, "I have seen all but one of the opposition and if I am any judge of horse-flesh then we should win by a distance."

He seemed so confident, as did my father, that even I, who was most cautious regarding such matters, was tempted to lay a bet. I said as much to Dan when he returned, but I was surprised by his reaction.

"The owner knows nothing of the opposition. If you must, take shorter odds on the mare being placed in the first two." His words were so convincing that I found myself taking note of the hints of this mere slip of a boy and, returning to my natural reluctance to commit myself, took his advice. My father however, placed such money as he had on a win, confident of the horse's chances.

The night before the heats, there was a dance on the heath. Gipsy fiddlers led the way and before long everyone was involved. I lifted my skirts and joined them. Changing partners at the end of every sequence, we skipped and pirouetted across the grass as darkness fell. John sat with my father, bemused by the whole business but captivated by the music. And when he was tired, he just lay down on the ground and slept.

At one point, I found I was partnering my own son.

27

Strangely, by the light of the fires, his hands looked brown, even the palms of them, but I took it to be a trick of the light and moved on. I'd not seen much of him since we had arrived and would not see much more of him the next day either. It was as if he had changed allegiance and was now supporting the rival camp.

It was late, very late before the music died down and the fires flickered low. We were exhausted. We slept in the open, too tired to consider what the weather might have chosen to throw at us. As it was, it was a fine and a warm night, and given the chance I know I would have slept well into the morning. Still it was early to rise, come the dawn. Horses needed attention. Our big day had arrived.

There were several races that day and plenty of excitement for my father. The grey gelding we had brought won a prize of ten guineas. The owner, a leading figure on Ipswich Borough Council was delighted. It seemed to augur well for our main event.

The parade of colours seemed to take forever. I was impatient; I just wanted to get it all started. I could hear my father giving his instructions to the jockey, resplendent in blue and white silk. The bay mare looked a picture of health.

The jockey was told to spare the horse in the first heat; not merely to underplay her finishing speed but to remember how far she might have to run in total that day. He was not to press her; simply to win, if necessary by the narrowest of margins.

But it was hard to rein her back; she was a natural racer and, once she hit the front, wanted to leave the opposition in her wake. She won the first heat with ease. Those in the watching crowd could sense her true strength, and from then on the odds shortened considerably.

As a result, Mr. Butler's bay mare became the clear favourite, to such an extent that little attention had been focused on the other four horses, who had been far less convincing.

It was one of these others, a brown gelding, that seemed to be the charge of Dan's new-found friends. Joseph Rose was involved in the training of the horse and Will Saunders was the jockey. Oddly, the horse looked familiar. You get used, when you work with horses, to recognising them, almost as you'd recognise people. The bearing, the stature, the canter, the gallop, reminded me of a gelding I'd seen at Beccles races earlier in the season; a fine beast, but with a white star on its forehead and white hooves. It had been a winner at that meeting. This horse however was completely brown, but there was enough about it to suggest a close kinship. I felt uncomfortable for my father, but glad for myself I had hedged my bets.

Huge crowds thronged the heath on race days. You could smell the foodstuffs for sale and the dung and the sweat of the horses. Colours dazzled you as all but the very poorest put on a show. A few beggars had made their way there but were soon driven off and replaced by musicians and traders, pedlars and entertainers.

Unbeknown to the authorities, games of Faro and Hazard were openly played, and many went home far poorer than when they arrived. You had to keep your pockets well buttoned down, as there were pickpockets aplenty. Even those with their wealth stitched into the seams of their clothes could not be sure to escape the most ardent and skilled of street thieves.

The second heat came quicker than we would have wished. There was no arguing about it. The Steward had used a half-hour glass to time it. Then came a blast on a trumpet to let us know it was time to race again. As was the way then, training grooms were encouraged to purge and sweat their charges to reduce their weight, but it sapped their strength too and the tactics had to be different this time. "Don't let her go too soon. Even if it means losing this heat, we'll be given a longer break before the third, so save her strength for that one."

Again five horses took to the field, but it was a closer contest this time. Racing then could be a bit of a bear-garden. The course was ill-defined and gipsy lads would canter their mounts alongside the racehorses. They were dressed in bright colours, so at times it was hard to tell which were the genuine contestants. There was a lot of bumping and barging. For safety's sake, our jockey held back, staying out of trouble, and at the last the brown gelding ridden by Will Saunders pulled clear. There was no need to chase a lost cause, so our mare came home with the pack, none the worse for a second outing. We weren't unduly concerned. We were just biding our time, we told ourselves confidently. The gelding had won a heat, but it was a far from convincing performance, and we knew our mare had so much more to show.

Suddenly, I heard a voice beside me. It was Dan.

"I hope you took my advice."

There he was, appearing again, like a bad penny and... his hands were brown. Nowhere near as brown as they had appeared the night before, but I hadn't been imagining it. Still, I put it to the back of my mind and concentrated on the next race.

For much of the time, though we were stationed on high ground, the pack would be out of our sight. As in the previous heats, there would be two circuits of approximately two miles. The horses had already completed eight miles and nobody was in a hurry to rush the start of the third heat. With renewed confidence, we watched our jockey resaddle. Cheers went up as the race began. I looked round. Again Dan had disappeared. As the horses went past at the end of the first circuit, our bay mare was comfortably placed just behind the pacesetter, the blue and white cap of the jockey clearly visible, followed closely by Will Saunders, dressed in green on the brown gelding.

For several minutes, we could not really make out how things were progressing, but as the horses began to accelerate into the last half-mile, you should have heard the roar. Though it was hard to discount the foreshortened view we were getting, it was plain our mare had hit the front and was clear of the field. The second win we had anticipated seemed ours for the taking. A shiver of excitement went through my father and I. We held hands, gripping ever tighter as they thundered towards us. This was how we had imagined it would be.

Then, from out of the pursuing group came a flash of green, and it was gaining on the blue and white of our mare. Suddenly, Will Saunders had conjured a burst of speed from his mount that was truly awesome. For a horse that had won less than thirty guineas before, this was quality that could not have been anticipated. Just as we had been close to celebrating success, it was wrenched away from us. That brown gelding, that no-one had given much thought to earlier, swept past our mare and took the prize.

I felt sick. My father looked worse. At least I would not lose money on the race. He stood to lose his money, his bonus and the respect of Mr. Butler who, though he took it like a true gentleman, could hardly disguise his disappointment.

As the brown gelding was led to receive the prize, I looked again at the unknown quantity that had proved such a remarkable success. And the more I looked at that horse, the more I could see in my mind the gelding with the white hooves and white star: no less could I see my own son's brown hands, and I knew... I knew what he had been a party to. I had heard of people disguising stolen champions to mop up prizes of thirty or fifty guineas. But this was the first time I had seen it for myself. I knew also I could not tell anyone of my suspicions. This was worse than breaking the law. This was breaking the law of the track and carried its own particular punishments. Too many had lost on a beaten favourite to let this go lightly. Bound bodies had been dragged from rivers for less. Blindings and shattered kneecaps were the currency of summary justice meted out by self-appointed guardians of fair play.

So I left it. And when I told Dan what I knew - not guessed, knew - you know what he said?

"I did warn you, so I don't know what you're so fussed about."

Then he put five sovereigns in my hand.

"That's your share," he said. "Good race, wun't it?"

Chapter 3
The words of Hannah Morse ~ 1725

I still feel guilty, though I know there is no reason why I should. I was never the guilty party in all this. A shopkeeper needs to keep on good terms with her customers and to prosecute one of their children is not a decision you arrive at lightly. I was certainly not used to finding myself in such a position. But they persuaded me it was necessary to put down this wave of crime that had blighted the town, especially involving the young. I was told, and I had to agree, that in order to prevent child thieves from moving into a life of criminal activity, they need an early lesson of the most impressive and instructional kind.

So it was when those two came to my shop just after May Day, I found myself in a dilemma. I had already told Master Malden, the joiner, that his son Dan was no longer welcome in my premises. A grocer cannot afford to accommodate the light-fingered. His visits to my shop had cost me dear. And me a poor widow too. On that occasion, he was accompanied by a girl. Whether she encouraged him, or he had her in tow to distract me, I cannot be certain. What I do know is this: one moment I had a fine ham, and the next it was gone and so were they. I can be fairly certain that the ham, found by the constable, being consumed by a gang of urchins beside the river was the very same ham that had only an hour earlier resided in my store. I cannot afford such a loss. I said as much to the boy's father and he was most apologetic as he had been on other occasions. He offered to pay for what had been lost, and that might have settled the matter had the constable not returned to instruct me regarding my duty.

I cannot afford theft of my goods. Neither can I afford to prosecute those who would steal them, even if that had been my intention. However, it was felt that it was time to make a stand. The watchmen, the constables and the civic leaders themselves had a point to make. I was not the only one suffering from the pilfering ways of Ipswich youths.

"I have been instructed to ask you to prosecute the two you say stole from your shop. They may be young, but a felony is a felony," the constable said.

I could hardly disagree.

"But to prosecute would demand money I do not have, even if it is for the benefit of the whole community as you suggest."

"I am again instructed to advise you to request a sum of ten pounds from the Borough to undertake the prosecution. That should cover the warrant for the arrest of Dan Malden and the girl Stephenson and ensure they be prosecuted before a jury."

So they made it easy for me. But I wasn't happy about it. I had to tell all I knew and swear before Mr. Cornelius that it was the truth. It felt like I was on trial. At the end of it all, I was guaranteed the ten pounds and I went to set the legal wheels in motion.

Later that evening, I heard a knocking at my door. It was hardly a surprise. Mary Malden was there, sobbing so hard, she could hardly contain herself.

"They've taken Dan. They say as he robbed your shop, he is to be prosecuted."

"Come in a minute." What more could I say?

I tried to explain. "I wasn't going to let it go any further than between us, but the constable was so insistent," I said. "If your boy goes on like this unchecked, it won't just be the Borough Court, it'll be the Assize and they'll send him to America... or worse."

"But what if they lock him up?" she cried. "He's thirteen. He'll not survive. Oh what on earth was he thinking of, taking a ham? It's not as though he's hungry or nothing. It's those other boys he's with; that's the trouble."

"Not only boys," I said. "There was a girl with him this time."

"Maud Stephenson?"

I nodded.

"She's the same age as him, and no better than she should be. And what use has he got yet for girls? - Look at him! - He's still a child."

I didn't like to say, "...but a child with the vices of a man." I couldn't voice my opinion to a distraught mother that, far from being led astray, Dan Malden seemed to do most of the leading, for all his lack of stature.

"Don't you worry: the Constable says as he's only little, he'll get a warning this time."

That had been the way the Constable had put it to me, though I had my doubts. If they wanted to make an example of him, it would not be by waggling the finger of admonishment. Still, she calmed down. We shared a pot of tea and I explained that whilst I could not change a word of my sworn statement, I would present the boy's good points to the court, and suggest they might temper the sentence with a dash of mercy.

Over the following days, people took sides. There were those who shunned my shop, feeling I had no right to behave so harshly to my neighbours. Others, mainly other shopkeepers, said it was about time these ruffians were taught a lesson and were wholly behind my actions. I remained unconvinced.

They held Dan Malden and the girl for a week or two, pending the swearing of a jury, and it must have been around the beginning of June that I was called to give my evidence. There were plenty of other accusations levelled at these two, but mine was the clearest of evidence, and I knew it was my word that would see justice done at the end of the day.

The Mayor was very pedantic regarding the process of the trial. It took an age. Twelve good men and true were finally sworn in. 'Trial by your peers' - They were more my peers than his. They were nearly all shopkeepers for a start. Men I'd known most of my life. John Toakley, Daniel Kerridge, Emannuel Abbitt - Good honest men, but with the same axe to grind as myself.

James Dobbs, John Beadman, Isaac Drake - They wanted an example made of shop thieves, and this one would do. Daniel Dale, Thomas Booth, John Boggis: they weren't missing a morning from work just to send somebody home with a ticking off. William Bedwell, Benjamin Dewy, John Harvey: you could see the determination on their faces to make these miscreants pay. Not enough were caught, so it was necessary to hit hard those that were. And our Mayor; he knew how to hit them hard.

The girl came out of it all right. She had tidied herself up a bit; looked like butter wouldn't melt. She had those twelve jurymen in the palm of her hand. And I couldn't really be sure what her part had been in the whole affair. In the end, she was found 'not guilty' and skipped out of court, light as air; until the next time.

Then came the judgement.

"Daniel Malden Junior: the jury say on their oath that you are guilty of the felony of which you are charged. Therefore it is ordered by this court that on Saturday the 5th day of June, between the hours of one and three, you be tied to the tail of a cart and by this dragged from the Town Gate up to the Mitre Tavern, and from there across the highway known as the Buttermarket, right up to the house called the King's Head, and from thence back to the prison, being whipped all the way."

Mary Malden gasped, then burst into tears.

Her husband called out, "But that is savagery!"

One or two in the court actually applauded. But the judgement was not yet over.

"…And then to custody for hard labour in the town work-house for a period of three months."

Even I was shocked by that! So too was the boy. All the colour drained from his face. This was an adult punishment for a regular offender. Yet it was being imposed upon a child at his first conviction, purely to teach the rest a lesson. I couldn't face Mary Malden. I just turned away and went home. The Maldens never came to my shop after that. And I never took joinery work to him.

It was not that we bore each other grudges, so much as we would have felt uncomfortable in each other's company.

So it was, on Saturday, after the hour of one in the afternoon, vengeance was practised in our town. I'd like to say they held back the flail on account of the boy's youth and small-ness of stature, but the idea was to show thieves what they could expect, and the boy's cries echoed around the Buttermarket. Crowds lined the street as though this were their Saturday enter-tainment, which of course it was. Some threw things; others jeered.

I heard they bathed his back with salt-water, but he bore the scars for the rest of his life. Maybe it was then he acquired his real hatred of authority, or perhaps it was there all along. Whichever is true, it didn't prove much of a lesson. By the time he came out of the Workhouse, he was toughened in many ways. Any innocence he may have had was gone. And looking back on it, I am sorry I was ever persuaded to play such a part in it. For everything that happened later may have had its roots there.

Chapter 4
The words of Thomas Brasier ~ 1727

It is possible that I was the only one that saw the good in Dan Malden... apart from his mother of course. She would never hear a word against him. But that's mothers for you. As far as I can see, when a mother gives birth to a child, she becomes utterly blind to his faults. And my daughter was no different from any other mother in that respect. I, on the other hand, knew only too well what I was taking on when I suggested the boy worked with me in the grooming and care of horses. However, I felt he had enough saving graces to make it worth my effort. Not that there weren't moments when I was almost prepared to give up on him.

Take, for example, that race at Bury when he conspired with Joseph Rose to win a race I should have won. Oh yes, I knew about that. My daughter thought it had escaped my notice, but you don't spend this number of years with horses not to recognise a ringer when you see it. And I let young Dan know how I felt just as soon as I could.

It was about a week later. We were well out of town, along the foreshore. From early morning, we had been exercising the horses. Most were not horses involved in racing. No, my major task was keeping the hunters fit so my master could furnish house guests with a range of mounts at a moment's notice. We had ridden down Gainsborough Lane and along the foreshore. The tide was out and otherwise impassable corners became negotiable. The late summer sun was high enough to throw a fair measure of warmth. The river rippled silver.

Leaving the shore at Nacton, we rode above the two great estate houses that loured over that part of the Orwell and came, by degrees, to Levington. Here beside the old church with its brick tower was an inn. The Ship was a favourite haunt for sailors and smugglers, but also attracted a number of gardeners and grooms.

Here was a chance for a drink and a chat and an exchange of news.

You could see clear down to the river from the front of the Ship. To the east, a track ran down to the creek where small boats would land at high tide. Other times, mud stretched as far as the central stream and was home to oyster-catcher and curlew. Some days, we would ride the horses as far as Walton, coming back across Trimley marshes.

That day, as I recall, we stopped at Levington, practising the horses up and down the slope between the Ship and the foreshore. I decided it was time for lunch and so we tethered the horses and ordered ale for them and ourselves. I've always been of the opinion that if a quart of ale can put the spring back in the step of a man, it can surely do as much for a horse. There were two other lads with me that day, but they sat apart from Dan and I. I felt it was time to tell him what I knew.

"Do you want to work with horses, Dan?"

"You know I do." He gulped at his beer.

"And you want to be a jockey - to ride in races for gentlemen?"

"Of course, just as soon as I am old enough."

"But how are we supposed to trust you?" I asked.

He came on all innocent.

"What do you mean?"

"I mean that deception you played the other day."

"The other day?" He gulped again at his beer.

"Did you really think I wouldn't recognise a trick like that?"

"But... mum..."

"Oh, she spotted it too, did she? Well that's no surprise. She is my daughter. You are just fortunate no-one else has been round asking you questions... and all to win a bet, no doubt. How much did you win by the way?"

He looked sheepish and crestfallen.

"... Rather less than I lost I assume. I will now tell you this. I have encountered the likes of Joseph Rose before. If that is

38

the company you wish to keep, then I pity you. You know he has spent time in Chelmsford Gaol on more than one occasion. And the word is that next time he will hang at Tyburn by way of Newgate."

He began to look more contrite, but I was not letting him escape my grasp that easily.

"You will pay me back: maybe not all I lost, but I will make you pay. For the next six months, you will work longer, and for less. But you will continue to give your mother her full allowance. That way, the only one to suffer in this shall be you."

He said nothing. But his eyes said it all. He was sorry. At that moment he was wholly penitent. I did not believe it would last, but it was something to work on for the time being.

It was a very subdued Dan Malden who rode back that afternoon; very subdued indeed. I only ever saw him like that one other time in his life. The day he left the Workhouse after his three months hard labour, he seemed a pale shadow of his former self. Skinny - you could see his bones in such a way that it appeared he had barely enough skin to cover his body. He had never been anything other than thin, but it was a shock to see him. If I had produced a horse like that, I would have been accused of cruelty - justifiably so. It took months to put back what they had taken from him both in body and spirit. And I like to think I played my part in restoring him to health. We all assumed he would change, and learn, and for a while there was every sign he would be a better man for the impositions that had been laid upon him.

In the summer of 1727, my daughter, Mary, had just given birth to the last of her five children, a daughter, Elizabeth. Dan was spending more time than ever with the horses. He was growing stronger and even showed a light down covering his upper lip. He was fast becoming a man. The desires and ambitions were growing in time with his body, which is just the way it should be.

My master was keen that I should see a colt that was for sale quite close to Ipswich. So it was that I took Dan with me to the estate they call Shrubland.

To the North of the Bury Turnpike just before the Norwich Road plunges North, buried in vast acres of woodland, was the home of Mr. Edmund Bacon. Not a racing man himself; nevertheless it was one of his grooms who had recognised the potential of a colt he had bred, and now it was for sale. My judgement in the matter would decide whether those I served would complete the purchase. It was unusual then to find locally bred horses with the mixture of speed and stamina necessary for racing. My master tended to prefer horses from the Vale of York, but by reputation, this colt was worthy of our attention.

So it was, we found ourselves, Dan and I, riding side by side, turning off the road and towards Shrubland Hall. It was like no place we had ever been - as soon as we had passed the gatehouse, it was like entering a netherworld. I had lived in Suffolk all my life, but the countryside was never like this. Once through a barrier of trees, rolling grassland stretched away to the near horizon, punctuated by mature limes, oaks and chestnuts. It was now high summer and the sweet chestnuts in their prickly coats seemed to offer themselves to all who might pass by. Sheep roamed, pheasants flocked; everywhere looked lush and good and plentiful. And it was silent. And it didn't smell - well, not the smells of the town and the river - just the damp grass and sheep dung smell, the smell of cedar and yew.

Here was a glimpse of old England before enclosure, before the forests were felled to build ships of war: a reminder of the way much of England must have been before a handful of men had become empowered to claim for themselves such islands of tranquillity. The stables lay to the North East of us as we approached. We knew them to be opposite the old hall, across a broad courtyard. But all this was shielded from our view, as yet.

The tracks leading in and out were in finer fettle than most of the roads into Ipswich. Holes had been filled with gravel and chalk and compacted to give an even surface, but with a patchwork appearance. To one side of the track, a sandy bank, almost a cliff, rose up. On the other were feeding pens for game. Deer ambled across the scene as though they expected to be a part of the landscape. It was hard not to feel envious. That one man could have so much!

Had I but known what I know now, I would have seen this was all a sham, a glossy exterior whilst within such places, often carpets and drapes were faded and almost threadbare, and they might have envied my small but cosy home.

There were no less than six ways out of that park, and each with a gatehouse to guard it. Riches come at a price and that price is protection. That rich man could no sooner wander freely in his own woods than I. Man-traps and spring guns lay in wait for the unwary rambler. Gamekeepers with flintlocks would shoot first; check whom they had shot afterwards. No, Mr. Bacon's hall was more of a prison and a trial to him than any home I ever lived in.

We were almost there before we were first challenged. I carried a letter of introduction, though it is doubtful whether the man enquiring as to our credentials could read it. He took us at our word and we were soon gazing on that we had come to see. The colt looked good enough, though light of limb and almost fragile. But of her speed there was no doubt and she had a fine pedigree. Given time to mature and the correct schooling, this was a horse any gentleman would be proud to own. I had taken Dan in order that he should see how I handled the negotiations. In the end I agreed to have the beast for a fair price, added to which I was led to believe a small gratuity would be mine. As it was likely such a bonus would also be forthcoming from my master, I felt this was a good day's work. It was arranged that I should send Dan to collect the horse a week later when all necessary arrangements had been made. Certificates indicating the age and breeding of the horse would need to be furnished, and at my master's stables appropriate accommodation found for such a horse.

I sent him off with a mind befuddled by instructions.

"You can read well enough to check the papers are complete. Ensure the colt is well watered before you ride him back, and light though you are, walk him up Whitton Hill and Spring Lane."

Still I continued... "Check his hooves. Too many owners knowing a horse is to be sold will leave aside shoeing, so by the time they part with him, you may need the services of a blacksmith before you can ride him. No, you check, and if he is shedding a plate, don't accept him until the farrier has seen to him."

Dan said yes to each instruction, clearly irritated by the fuss I was making. What I wanted him to see was that attention to detail is important. I was trying to make that abundantly clear. The last reminder was to take charge of the gratuity I had been promised for handling the deal. The exact sum had not been agreed but I had hopes of at least five guineas. Finally, Dan left me. The Coddenham carrier would take him to the entrance. He could walk the rest of the way. He could have ridden and led the colt back, but you never know how one highly-strung animal will respond to another. It seemed safer this way. I expected him back by dusk at the latest.

By sunset, when the rest of the horses were at rest and I was thinking of returning to my own home, Dan had not appeared. I was concerned. Of course I was concerned. I thought of all the dangers that could befall travellers, even if their journey was as short as this. Had he chanced to take a short cut through the woods and fallen prey to the keepers' guns? Had highwaymen or foot-pads attacked him along one of the two open stretches before he reached the town? Or had he taken my gratuity and drunk himself stupid in the Maypole or some other hostelry along the way. Oh yes, I had no illusions about Dan: make no mistake. I began to curse myself for not playing safe and collecting the colt myself.

Just as I was about to give up on him, calm as you like, in he trotted. The colt was breathing heavily and had worked up quite a sweat. I was none too pleased. What I did not understand was how, if he had ridden so hard, had it taken him so long to get back.

"Where have you been all this time and why have you

ridden the colt so hard?

"Oh, I stayed longer than I intended and had to hurry back." He grinned the way he did when he felt he was putting one over on someone.

He drew out the paper work and it was then I noticed two small bags hanging from his belt. One he gave to me.

"Your gratuity, like you expected."

I glimpsed inside. Instead of the five or six guineas I expected, there were ten. He grinned again, as if to say, 'didn't you trust me?' Well, actually, no I didn't - even then.

"Don't you worry about the colt," he said. "I'll see he's comfortable. Get you on home - see you in the morning."

And so I went, more confused than ever, wondering what was in the other bag jangling at his belt, and how he had come by it.

It was about a week later I was able to put together the fragments of information that held the answers. Up on the heath above Ipswich, you find all sorts. There are usually gipsies and tinkers: travelling menageries camp there too. There are a few scattered dwellings - some of them date back to the time of the great plague when pest houses were erected for the sick and dying. There are a couple of beer houses that service the needs of drovers and shepherds, farmers and keepers.

You never know who you will meet up there, but one thing is certain: it is a fine place for news and gossip. Word was that a young man in a jockey's cap had laid a challenge in sovereigns that his horse would outride any there. Two gentlemen, believing they might teach this upstart a lesson took up the challenge. Young though the lad was, and the beast he was riding also, but according to the tales I heard, that combination of youth flew like the wind and left the two gentlemen sorely out of pocket.

Now it all made sense... the length of time taken, the horse arriving in the state it did and the money Dan had clearly come back with. He had obviously seen fit to placate me with an enhanced gratuity.

But it hadn't entirely been a chance encounter. No, there

was no reason why he should have come back by such a devious route. He had gone there seeking such a contest. The colt was, as far as anyone in the neighbourhood knew, an unknown quantity, and he had spotted a perfect way to make a winning wager. For all that, it was my gratuity that had formed the basis of his wager and someone else's horse that was being stretched to its limits. Still it was hard to feel really angry with him. There was a quickness of wit about Dan Malden that said to you, "This lad will either be a wealthy man one day, or he will end his days at the end of a rope."

Chapter 5
The words of Dan Malden ~ 1728

By the time I was sixteen, I felt I knew all there was to know about life. Certainly my parents believed me worldly-wise to such an extent I was beyond their control. The truth of the matter was I was quite innocent regarding most things and found then, as later, others I trusted were only too keen to take advantage of the fact.

It seemed as though I had been waiting forever for my first ride as a jockey. I knew I had it in me. I had experienced the rush of excitement you get riding an animal at full gallop. I worked well with horses and those that knew me responded without my use of the whip.

Several of the horses I handled had been successful in races and challenges. I knew their owners must have looked at their own paunchy bodies and then looked at me. I could ride under the lowest weight, yet I was strong enough to handle the most headstrong beast. So why was I having to wait so long to ride in earnest. They must have known I could ride winners. I was certainly anxious to prove I could.

My chance finally came just after an event that went wrong. Mr. Butler's son-in-law had accepted a challenge of several hundred guineas to ride two heats from Six Mile Bottom to the top of Cambridge Hill at Newmarket and then the return. The first heat was an arduous course - six miles, mostly uphill. The horse had to be taken there days in advance. Still in his twenties, the fool insisted on riding himself. But a diet of red meat, port and sweet puddings in abundance had left him in poor condition to take on such a contest. He was not so much beaten as humiliated. Losing by a distance, the second heat was never required. As a result, my chance came soon after.

It was at a lesser meet, held at Elmswell. Prizes for the set races were small, but challenges and wagers could mean large sums could still change hands. The mare so humbled at Newmarket was seen by many as a loser. I knew better. The two gentlemen I rode against that day were fine enough horsemen but they weren't to know that the mare I rode possessed qualities of speed and endurance that had been masked in her earlier outing. We came home a good three lengths clear and my reputation was established. I felt the world was mine for the taking.

At sixteen, other urges began to assert themselves. I wasn't totally innocent where girls were concerned, but such experiences I had gained were mere childish fumblings. I was, as yet, untouched by love. In my wilder days there had been every opportunity to learn what men and women do. On the banks of the Orwell on a summer's evening, girls like Maud Stephenson were only too keen to exhibit themselves - even when there wasn't a lot to exhibit. There was more humour than desire on our part. It was something to joke about amongst the boys.

Late at night, after sailors spilled from the dockside bars with their whores, you could watch their coupling in alleyways and riverside shacks. On one occasion, a whore was left drunk and incapable where she lay after the tar had finished with her. One or two of the older lads amongst us availed themselves of what was on offer. I didn't as I recall. I couldn't get excited about it and didn't see the point. But then I was still very young. Just about all of the girls I knew had older lads in tow. I was smaller than most and girls paid scant regard to me.

In high summer, sometimes you could earn extra money by helping to bring in the harvest. If you walked just beyond the town boundaries, you could find temporary employment. On days that I was not needed with the horses, I would take myself off to Whitton or Brightwell. Sometimes, a farmer would look at the size of me and scoff, but when he saw the work I could do, he would realise I was worth my day's pay.

It was in August 1728 that I met Alice. She was daughter of the farm foreman and must have been a year or two younger than me. For all that she had a fine full figure and she smiled at me whenever I looked at her. We were stooking corn; tying it in bundles, behind the reapers.

"You work with horses, you say?"

"I'm a jockey," I said proudly.

"Go on - only rich gen'lemen ride in races."

"Not if they've got someone who's a better horseman, they don't."

"So why are you here?"

"My grandad - he's the head groom - he's sold a number of the older horses and the new ones haven't arrived, so there's less work to do at the stables."

She grinned. "When we get a break, you can sit with me if you like."

I did like. I liked the idea a lot. So I set to work with a will, half-believing that the quicker we finished that corner, the sooner the break would arrive.

"Can I come and see the horses?" she asked. I don't think she really believed me.

"Of course, just as soon as you have the time."

She grinned again, undid a lace or two on her bodice and continued, matching me stook for stook.

When we did take a break, we ambled down to the stream at the foot of the slope and splashed the cool clear water first over ourselves, then over each other.

Laughing I chased her to a bank out of sight of the rest and grabbed hold of her. She didn't resist. Far from it. The moment was altogether too short; a few minutes of kisses and touches and caresses. I didn't really know what I was doing, but my touches seemed to please her, and hers certainly pleased me. That was all it was - kisses and touches, but it truly beat anything Maud Stephenson had to offer and I knew by the end of the day that I was in love.

Alice came to the stables later that week. I was proud to show her that I hadn't been boasting. I had ridden winners in three of my five races and was a respected member of the stabling team. She came home with me for a meal, after which I walked her slowly back. It was still just light when I bade her goodnight. And always with her, there was kissing and loving with a passion, though she always made it clear there were limits to how far it would lead. I was happy to go along with that. I loved Alice: I think I probably always did in a way. Taking all the women I knew after her, including the two I claimed to have loved, not one of them got to me the way Alice did in the summer of 1728.

There were some weeks when I saw very little of her: work kept me busy at the stables and I would come home exhausted. It was late in September when I left off a little earlier than usual: I decided after a gap of several days, I needed to see Alice. I tidied myself up and took myself off to the farm. Their cottage was across the meadow from the big house where the farmer and his family lived. When I reached Alice's house, she wasn't there and her parents seemed rather evasive. Assuming she couldn't be far away, I went in search of her. Fond memory took me to the field where we had met and down toward the stream at its foot. As chance would have it, I heard sounds from the bank where we had first embraced. It was clearly the favourite spot of someone else. Something told me one of the voices was all too familiar. Of course, it was Alice. I didn't know then who her partner was but it was oh so clear that he had achieved a state of intimacy denied to me.

I still feel embarrassed by the events that followed. The young man - older than me, taller than me; by his clothes, richer than me - chuckled as he left us, still fastening himself as he walked cockily away. Alice, for her part, seemed unchastened, unconcerned.

"You didn't really think I meant it when I said I wanted to stay a virgin?"

Well, yes, I did. That was how innocent I was. I learned later it was the farmer's son. His name was Roland. I couldn't really hate him. Though I did finally wreak a small revenge on him, it was Alice I couldn't forgive. She was the one for whom I reserved my most bitter thoughts.

Roland received his small come-uppance soon after at the Ipswich Autumn Race Meeting. I had one race only, and my part in the event was small. This gave me the chance to renew old acquaintances.

"Joseph Rose - I've not seen you in a long while." I said. "And who is this beautiful lady?"

Looking very prosperous, Rose was now accompanied by a lovely girl who looked kind of familiar.

"Don't you recognise me, cousin?" she said.

I wasn't sure, but I still had memories of this girl who had visited our home a few times when I was small. I cast my mind back. There had been so many relatives on my mother's side of the family: I couldn't work out which one this must be.

"Think of your mother," she smiled.

"Of course, you're Mary Brasier - the one with the same name as my mother before she married my father." And then I thought... "but didn't you get sent to...?"

"Prison, you were going to say. Oh yes, but that wun't so bad. And it did have its compensations."

"What Mary means," interjected Joseph Rose, "is that is where we met. And as soon as we were both able to leave our town house, so to speak, we decided to work together."

"You look... prosperous," I said.

"That is because a little prosperity has seen fit to drop our way," Joseph Rose confirmed. "With Mary's charm and my ideas, things is looking up, so to speak."

"I'm riding later today," I informed him.

"And is this a race I should put money on?"

"Not on my horse. Not unless you want to lose," I said. I know the other horses and unless they are out of sorts, I'd not reckon my chances. On the other hand," I boasted, "I may be so brilliant that I can coax a win out of a decidedly inferior horse. You never know - but I'd keep my money safe if I was you."

"Then we'll just have to make our fortune some other way."

"Joe's got a great way to part fools from their money," laughed Mary.

Now that interested me. I was still smarting from what I saw as Alice's betrayal. I knew Roland was at the race-meeting and if ever a fool needed parting from his money it was he. I suggested as much to Joe.

"You just point him out and we'll skin him," he said. "Seeing as he's a friend of yours, I suggest you get him away from his friends - it makes it easier to pick 'em off one at a time."

"I wouldn't exactly call him a friend, but I'll see what I can do."

"Before you do, let me just explain how this works, so to speak."

And then, at length, Joseph Rose explained his latest money-making scheme. It involved three people and the knowledge that one particular horse certainly would not win. How he could be sure of that I did not like to ask. There are few reliable ways of just making a horse run slowly. There are, however, many ways of making a horse unlikely to finish a race. Most of those result in the death of the unfortunate animal. Nothing on earth would have prompted me to become involved in that kind of arrangement.

A short while later, spotting Roland with his farmer friends, I made my way over to him. He seemed to have another girl in tow. At first, I don't think he recognised me, but when I mentioned having met him at the foot of Dales Meadow, he was naturally anxious to put space between himself and his companions. I played my part, saying that I bore him no hard feelings and I wished him well with Alice. It was clear she played no significant part in his life, but was a convenient port of call from time to time.

Then up strode Joseph Rose. He thrust a pile of sovereigns in my hand.

"There you are Mr. Malden. Didn't I say it couldn't lose? I'm only sorry you hadn't the means to bet more on such a horse."

To say that Roland was amazed would be an understatement. What happened next was to compound that amazement.

"I will consult the source of all wisdom and you might as well keep that to place on my behalf on the next race," I said.

At that I beckoned Mary to join me. "I don't think you've met my cousin, Mary," I said to Roland.

"Delighted to meet you," said Mary suddenly softening her vowels and sounding, as well as looking, the part.

"Mary, dear cousin," I said, "as you informed me so accurately as to the winner of the last race, could you be so kind as to tell me what will win the next?"

I turned to Roland. "My cousin is very close to (and here I raised my eyebrows as if to intimate the declaration of a closely guarded secret) the owners of the finest horses running here."

"Well," Mary began, "it hardly seems fair to wager on a certainty, but…"

"Go on…" said Roland.

"Is he with you?" asked Mary as if reluctant to reveal her confidences to someone she didn't know.

"Oh yes, Roland is a friend." I said. "No hard feelings." And I shook him by the hand.

"The race will soon be off sir," said Joe.

We all looked at Mary. "Well, as I said. A certainty it is, so Mr. Drury's gelding will win without the shadow of a doubt."

"Bless you," I cried and kissed her. Then turning to Joe, I said, "Take all my winnings from before and place them on Mr. Drury's grey gelding."

Joseph Rose turned as if to hurry away and follow my instructions.

" Uh, before you go…" called out Roland.

"I'm sorry sir, but I've got to lay a bet for Mr. Malden here."

"Oh if Roland wants to lay a sovereign or two," I said, "surely you can take that at the same time."

"Well, he'll have to hurry sir," said Joe.

"A certainty, you say?" asked Roland.

"A shame to accept the winnings I'd say," said Mary.

"Alright then..." He fished into the lining of his jacket and produced a purse with at least thirty guineas in it."

"Are you sure, sir?" asked Joe.

"Of course I'm sure. It's little more than this... jockey is laying out. A certainty - I'll have some of that if you don't mind. Now get a move on, my man, or we'll all lose out."

Within moments, Joseph and Mary melted away with the money Roland assumed was mine and a good deal more that was formerly his. He was not unduly concerned until the racing certainty proved to be anything but. I, of course, appeared to accept my losses like a gentleman. Poor Roland was nearly in tears.

"I thought you said it was a certainty."

"So I believed it was, but that's racing for you."

"But all that money - aren't you bothered to the point of distraction?"

"Easy come, easy go," I answered, trying desperately to conceal my glee at his discomforture. And there I left him, a poorer but wiser man. I didn't see him or his deceivers for some time after that. I did however see Alice, though it still pained me to do so. She appeared from time to time in the company of assorted young men. By Christmas she was growing around the waist and the last I heard she had married a common labourer and was living in poverty in Bramford. It was no more than I felt she deserved.

For a while, I put my energies into what I saw as my future. There were events for which to prepare horses. Sometimes, races at faraway places like Bungay and Thetford could occupy weeks of my life. The rules might require a horse to be stabled at a place as much as a fortnight before a race. Protecting the horses from the unscrupulous could be a full time job. Locked feeding troughs were little defence against determined characters. Many a night I slept beside a restless horse miles away from home. It was probably a relief for my parents. With five children in a small cottage, it was always going to be cramped. My absence, and with my sister about to go into service, it had to be easier for them. I still saw my mother received her just dues. I was being better paid now and the occasional purse for a successful ride made me feel like a king. I made a little on wagers of one sort or another and if I had known a touch more sense, I'd probably have lived a comfortable life. If only...

My greatest opportunity to date came when another local owner, Mr. Burroughs, accepted a challenge that was a little out of the ordinary. I had been seen riding at Ipswich, where I had ridden to success in four hard fought heats. This time, I was to compete at Beccles in a selling plate worth about twenty guineas to the winner. By way of a prize, there was also a large Montief and a silver salver - the kind of thing that attracted those for whom the money was but a small consideration. When it came to the race, the horses were very evenly matched and I really believe it was my slightness of stature that won it in the end. If you ride a series of heats, you are bound to lose a bit of weight in the process. I had less to lose than most. I can afford to have a good meal after weighing and it not affect the performance either of myself or the horse I am riding. Others anxious about not carrying extra pounds will go to a race half-starved and begin to lose strength after a couple of heats. Also, when you are weighed in after the race, if you have lost more than a couple of pounds, questions may be asked by the Steward. I have seen big men sweat off four full pounds in a race, and have success taken from them by judges who believe they have discarded weights from the saddle on the way round.

This was a case like that, and it worked to my advantage. After the four heats, two of us had exactly the same results. Before a deciding heat was to be run, we were weighed, and the rotund gentleman could not draw the weight. He was found to be a remarkable six pounds lighter. It was a hot day and no-one was going to actually accuse a gentleman of cheating. But he was expected to accept defeat, which naturally, he did. He was a renowned horseman and though I won by default, it was a win that attracted the attention of others.

Mr. Burroughs, in the meantime was divided in his mind over his success. He won the twenty guineas, though three came my way, two went to the clerk to help maintain the course, and a further two to the poor of the town. However, the horse, a favourite of his daughter's, according to the rules, had to be sold for twenty guineas. The race participants threw dice to see who should acquire the horse at such a price. In the end, to placate his daughter, Mr. Burroughs had to buy back the beast from its purchaser, leaving him out of pocket on the day. And he wasn't even a betting man.

So it was that a message arrived requiring my services to ride the renowned 'Firedragon' in a long-distance contest between Bungay and Norwich. Three horses were taking part in a challenge that carried a prize of two hundred guineas. Mine was the clear favourite. Permission had been obtained from my employers. I was to leave for Bungay right away.

No sooner had I arrived than I was taken over the course by a local horseman. Clearly disappointed that he had not been chosen to ride Firedragon, he was stiffly polite but a little short with me. Nevertheless, he knew the area and I was able to pick up the local knowledge I lacked. When it came to the event itself, I could hear his voice in my head as we raced, and his advice proved invaluable. The fourteen miles or so we would cover would be from Bungay Common to Trowse Hall. The race had drawn a great deal of interest and crowds were to flock around significant points of the course, especially the start and finish.

There was much fussing from the head groom, though the

owner himself seemed unconcerned and kept his distance. Large sums were being placed in bets. Other events were also being staged: coursing at Bungay and a main of cocks in an inn yard close to Norwich. Traders had appeared as if from nowhere and set up stalls on the common near the start. It was a fine autumn day and carriages had brought people from Diss and from Lowestoft and the countryside around..

The signal to start was the dropping of a kerchief, and away we sped. Up Hollow Hill we paced with little between us. None of us was prepared to set a pace with such a distance still to go. As we approached the open expanse of Dichingham Park, the riders separated, each preferring to choose his own line. The magnificent new hall stood in front of us. I chose to pass it to the right, leaving plenty of ground between myself and the long lake at the foot of the hill. I had been warned it was marshy down there and though a more direct route, it could slow down my mount and tire her. For all that, there were rabbit holes as we crossed the warren and I feared her catching a foot in one and throwing me or damaging the mare. But she was too clever and fleet of foot for that, and we crossed the park without mishap, passing Hedenham Church. From there it was mostly uphill to Brooke House. Sometimes in our part of the world, you can navigate from steeple to steeple, but I had been warned that to do so would draw me away from the most direct route. Norfolk churches can be surprisingly far from the centre of their parish. To a large extent, the fastest route would never stray far from the road and though it was uneven and rutted, the grassed areas on either side offered ample opportunity to stay free from trouble. The winter rains had not yet turned the route into a five-yard wide quagmire.

The going was as good as could be expected. At Hedenham, we had forded one stream: at Poringland we encountered another. There is the temptation to rush at such places: you are galloping downhill and they always look shallower than they really are. One of my opponents learned this to his cost and was abruptly deposited in the water. Though he was able to remount quite quickly, it had cost him dear. The remaining two of us were half a furlong away and he would have the discomfort of wet clothes for the rest of his ride. We moved again into open country, much of which was wooded. Having been led over the course, I had already decided my line, and found I was out of sight of my remaining contestant. At one point, we plunged down, then steeply up as we approached the last two miles.

Suddenly I was aware of the grey, well to my left, beginning to make a surge for home. Having reached the crest of the hill, the spires and towers of Norwich lay before us. It was an inspiration to give Firedragon the little encouragement she needed. We were in pursuit and gaining. I had been warned that she was no jumper and could see why my opponent had chosen the route he had. It meant clearing a fence or two, but he had a more direct line to Trowse Hall. I knew to be patient. I watched the grey peck on landing once and almost fall. The gentleman riding her would be more wary now and was looking for gaps or lower jumps. Better still, I was riding a creature with a reputation for conjuring up speed in the final mile of a race. If this mare was all she was supposed to be, then she would have pace to spare, and our final dash along the river would prove crucial. So it was to be. When my opponent began to tire, Firedragon seemed to grow in strength and with a furlong to go, we swept past as if the previous mile had not existed. To the cheers of large sections of the crowd, we crossed the finish.

I was sixteen years old and I had fine gentlemen shaking me by the hand. The owner of Firedragon arrived some hours later and slapped me on the back as though I were his greatest friend. I had to recount every inch of my ride and have it written down for posterity. I might be the centre of attention again a number of times in my life, but never would I enjoy such approbation from those bred to be my betters. They would be the ones later to shun me, to condemn me, to damn me. But at least, I had my moment. I had my moment!

Chapter 6
The words of 'Mudge'
(later to be known as Mary Malden) ~ 1728 & 1729

The first time I saw Dan Malden, he was full of himself. It was in one of those large coaching inns in the middle of Ipswich; the Greyhound most probably. It was not one of my usual haunts. I'd always been a sailor's girl and was better known in the Angel or the Half Moon. That night however, I was seeking solace. My man who had failed to show for some months should have been back. I'd just learned that he'd jumped ship in Marseilles and last been seen in the arms of some Frenchy girl. The last thing I needed was some tar coming on to me assuming he'd carry on where my man left off. So I dressed up nice-like. I may not be in the first flush of youth, but I can still look good if I take the trouble. Dan Malden noticed me, and was attracted, so I can't have looked too heartbroken.

He had quite a crowd around him - all classes - keen to hear how he'd just ridden from one place I'd never been to or heard of to another. I wasn't very impressed to be honest. 'Silly little squit,' I thought. Then he stopped explaining how clever he'd been and came over to where I was sitting.

"Wass your name, gal?" he asked.

I told him, "I 'in't your gal."

Then he turned all polite, which caught me by surprise, and even apologised like he meant it.

"My name is Mary, if you really want to know."

"What, another one - every woman I know is called Mary, practically."

"My friends call me Mudge," I said.

"Mudge it is then."

"I said my friends called me that, not just any little ol' squit I meet."

57

"I'd like to be your friend, Mudge, on account of the fact I've taken a fancy to you. And I'd like to think you might take a fancy to me."

I looked at him and laughed. He looked little more than a boy, and shorter than me by several inches. He must have been ten years younger than I was, and not a bit like the men I'd known.

"You might laugh," he said, but this week, real gen'lemen have clapped me on the back and shook my hand. They weren't so high and mighty as to lord it over me that I'm young or small in stature. They appreciated me for what I am and what I can do, and I'll tell you what, Mudge, give me half a chance and I'll be as much a man to you as any you've ever known."

I resented that. "And what makes you think I've known that many men?"

Then he smiled. "I've seen you down the Quay. You've never looked short of company."

"So why do you think I'm interested in talkin' to you when so many men have taken a shine to me. I could be down at the quay with any number of men."

"Maybe you could, but you 'in't," he grinned, "so with no better offer, you might accept mine."

To be honest, I wasn't sure what his offer was, but he clearly had money in his pockets that night, and while I've never stooped to selling myself, such talents as I might be prepared to share, I'd rather share with a man of means. In truth, there were no other offers available, and he was about as far from the tar that had abandoned me as he could possibly be. By my reckoning, that had to be to his advantage.

The one thing that I remember most about that night was what was to become almost an obsession with him. We walked through a churchyard as we made our way to my lodgings. A few stones marked the resting places of the great and mighty; otherwise, it was flat and grassy, except in one corner where a new grave had been dug and was still awaiting its recipient.

"You see there," he said, "just think of all those people

buried under here and nobody remembers who they were." He paused while I took it in. "I may not have a stone to mark my place when they stick my body in the ground, but they will remember me!" That was it - he wanted above all to be remembered - not to be famous and celebrated as such; but to leave a memory that would not easily fade.

"Look at my father," he said as we sat together, "or my grandfather if you like. However well they do what they do, who will remember them a century from now? I'll tell you one thing, Mudge, they will remember me. It may be for all the wrong reasons, but they are not going to forget who I am!" He said it with such surety and vigour, I could not doubt it, and though I am unclear where this idea came from, it persisted all the years I knew him.

So it was that after a few drinks and further recounting of his recent successes, I walked with Dan Malden down towards my lodgings. I didn't intend to give myself to him that night but he was good company and I was lonely. He was only a kid and in the end I think I was doing both of us a favour. And at the end of the night just before he slipped away to attend to his blessed horses, he kissed me. He thought I was still asleep.

"At least," I thought to myself, "he'll not be leaving me for some tart in a foreign port."

After that, we spent many nights together. He was so young and innocent, but he didn't mind when I put him right about things. He even said 'thank-you' sometimes. But what might have seemed right all turned very sour the day my sailor man, Jack, came home. I heard he was looking for me, and I was worried for Dan's sake. Jack can be a violent man, especially with drink inside him. In the end he found me and I, fool that I was, I went back to him. Decent men and me don't really mix, you see. It wasn't till Dan Malden changed his ways and became as much a rogue as any of them that I really loved him. Right then, I was Jack's lady and though we never actually married as such, it was understood that we were like man and wife.

When he went to sea again, I had to promise that I wouldn't resume relations with Dan. It was a promise I intended to keep, though I did keep an eye on his progress. It was a progress that was soon to take a downward turn.

Such money as he had must have rapidly disappeared. He could be seen regularly with a whore on his arm and frequenting the quayside inns. Perhaps it was to demonstrate to me that he didn't care. In a way, it just showed all the more that he did. He drank a lot too - not just table beer, but the strong stuff. I heard that there were times when he was unfit to ride. Then these two characters turned up. They were strangers to me but others identified them as Joseph Rose and Mary Brasier. Some said that they were part of a gang that were responsible for a deal of crime in Essex. They seemed drawn to racing like moths to a flame. There was a lot of money involved and from what little I understood, crooked dealing thrived.

It was high winter, about the middle of February, when I heard that my man Jack would not be coming home. I did not want to know all the details. Suffice it to say, he had killed a man in a brawl in a Low Country port. They do terrible things to prisoners over there. I heard they broke him on the wheel before finally putting him out of his misery. When I'd cried myself out, I pulled myself together and went in search of Dan again. It wasn't difficult to find him. It also wasn't difficult to prise him away from the dubious company he was now keeping. After all, he could get from me for free what he was paying others to supply.

It would be nice to be able to say that we picked up where we had left off, but he had changed. Gone was the innocent charm, and the pride in what he might hope to achieve. He had turned into yet another of the world's takers. He now had no illusions about me any more and whilst he appeared glad I was back, the warmth and tenderness had seeped out from his personality. His work had been going badly. The drink had affected his riding. Also, there had been doubts expressed when one of Mr. Butler's horses had died just before an important outing. Arsenic in the feed trough had been suspected, but never proved. Dan's past record was the only thing that had allowed him to remain working at the stables. But from then on he was kept away from caring for the finest horses and it was unlikely he would be chosen to ride them any more.

We began living together as man and wife soon after we got back together. It was not the way his parents wanted but as he said, not being taken to church and baptised as a child hadn't done him any harm, so what was the purpose in a church marriage? I still called myself Mrs. Malden if anyone asked.

One early march day, soon after noon, I went with Dan to the Black Boy. We met with three men I had not encountered before. Later, Joseph Rose and his woman joined us. I never liked her. I can't say why; I just felt uneasy in her presence: like she would encourage men to involve themselves in crime but stay clear of danger herself. I won't say I'm any sweet little thing where stepping over the legal line is concerned. I've done my share of theft, of handling and worse besides. But with Mary Brasier, you always felt it was the men around her who would hang and she would walk away unscathed. In the end, it wasn't quite like that, but nearly so. The names of the other three in attendance that day were given to us as Abraham Browne, Robert Green and John Smith, if you believe that. Browne, Green and Smith - innocuous and forgettable names for innocuous and forgettable characters. It seemed that they were part of a horse-stealing gang in Norfolk. Somewhere they had come into contact with Joseph Rose, who by then was already working with Thomas Rowden, an Essex pewterer, selling horses stolen from other parts of the country. The plan was to steal a few of the finest horses around, disguise them, and with the aid of false papers run them in races far enough away not to give rise to suspicion.

My fear was that Dan, being already suspect, would be the first arrested should any horse in his keeping be stolen. The plan, however, was more devious than that. What was required of Dan was his knowledge of other gentlemen's establishments. He had, after all, been to many of them and knew well which were easiest approached and which were least well protected. It was not expected that Dan's own charges would disappear in the night. So we were led to believe.

Plans emerged over days, in between which time, anecdotes were exchanged and confidences revealed. Joseph Rose and his woman seemed to know Dan from some past schemes they had been involved in together. That surprised me. I'd assumed his past was fairly unblemished. That just shows what a poor judge of character I was. And him coming from such a nice family too!

Ours was always to be a stormy relationship. That day would see it at its worst. I was unhappy about the arrangement he seemed to be getting himself into. The three Norfolk men did not inspire confidence. They seemed slow-witted and careless; not the kind to be involved with. Horse-stealing was, and probably always will be, a capital offence. As for the other scheming pair, their plans started simple enough but little by little they'd wheedle their recruits into taking on ever more dangerous roles. What had begun with Dan merely advising the gang where to steal from had become his leading them there. I could see that very soon he would become one of them, and it didn't take much imagination to envisage those three dimwits, at the first sign of capture, saving their own skins by offering Dan up as the organiser of the scheme. I said as much to him later that day once we had set another time to meet. He was angry, scornful of my fears and contemptuous of me.

"Since when did you get so fussy where my money comes from?" he yelled. "Perhaps you'd rather I lived on the scraps thrown by my high and mighty masters. Perhaps you'd like me to go crawling back to my parents so you'd be free to shake your tits at any sailor fresh in dock with money in his pocket."

That got me angry. "You think so much of that Essex lout and his strumpet, you'd try to walk on water for them."

"That strumpet as you call her is my cousin. Maybe you'd

like to shout abuse at all my family while you're at it."

The funny thing was, I liked Dan's family. His parents and their youngsters were like the family I never knew. I'd never known my father, and my mother died young, leaving me to have to learn to fend for myself from early on. No, what he said was unfair. So much of what he said was unfair. In the end, I shouted as loud as he did, in not too diplomatic words.

"You're too stupid to see you're being used. Joseph Rose will abandon you to the courts and disappear back to Essex. Six months ago you were doing well. It could still happen... your being a jockey and all that. It'll just take a bit of time to get people to trust you again. And if you want to do a bit of underhand stuff, do only such as leaves you in the clear when the constables come calling. Don't go emptying stables in the dead of night. That's a clear road to the gallows."

He sneered. "An' you never took nothin' what weren't yours, I s'pose. Them rich buggers are goin' to get all what's comin' to them, and I don't need some whinging sow to put me right about how I should live my life."

And then he slapped me. I fell to the floor, shocked and sobbing. I shouldn't have been surprised, really. I've always been drawn to men that knocked me about. It had always seemed part of the arrangement. But with Dan it had been different and I suppose the only thing that had attracted me to him, little squit that he was, was that he wasn't like the other men I'd known. Discovering he was just the same as all the rest knocked all the power from me. I picked myself up and I walked away from him. That's right. I left him, for the second time. The rest of what happened over the next few weeks I learned from his grandfather a month or two later.

Thomas Brasier came to see me. Fortunately I was on my own at the time. It was early evening and already dark. I was preparing a little food. Needing to make myself some money, I had resorted to carrying hot meals to the town watchmen. They'd sit through the night in their sentry boxes as a deterrent to thieves and drunken revellers. It was a thankless task. They were widely abused. It could be hard staying awake, but a good-looking woman offering a bit to eat and a kind word was more than they could refuse. Oh, there were those about the town who would mock.

"Get her in your box and give her a good seeing-to," they'd shout.

But most of these watchmen were old enough to be my grandfather. I felt sorry for them and they were usually grateful enough to see it was worth my while. I remember one night when I was down by Stoke Bridge and some youths had tipped over the sentry box trapping the poor man inside. He was probably dozing at the time and hadn't heard them coming. I chased them off and freed him from his predicament. He was almost in tears, poor man. He was only there for the protection of the people in this town, though I can hardly say knowing a watchman was near at hand would make me feel more secure than if he had not been there at all.

That was my night work. Added to that I took in laundry. And I did have occasional male visitors. After Dan left, it dawned on me that with all the men I'd known, I'd never fallen for a child - not since I was very young - but that's another story. It wasn't as if I'd been overly careful. No, I suppose there are those that can't create children and it looked as if I was one of them. So there was no need to be cautious, though I liked to believe I was at least a little choosy. To be honest, when Mr. Brasier arrived, I thought he was a customer. He was well dressed and looked slightly uncomfortable to be seeking out a woman that lodged alone. I had only ever seen him in his stable livery.

When I realised who he was, I guessed he had come on behalf of Dan and sat myself down to listen to what he had to say. Parts of the story I knew, of course, but so much more did he have to tell that I was still listening more than an hour later, and the food for the watchmen had dried up in the pan. They would go hungry that night.

There had been quite an epidemic of horse-thieving that must have begun soon after Dan and I had parted. Give him his due, Dan had used his intelligence and kept his head down, working quietly and without complaint. But at night, he had undoubtedly played his part in the thefts. It had crossed Thomas Brasier's mind that many of the victims had been stables that he and Dan had visited during the previous year. It had all come to a head when two fine thoroughbreds were taken from Mr. Butler's own collection, and inside knowledge assumed.

Thomas Brasier had confronted Dan and refused to believe his protests of innocence. In the end, he had admitted that he had helped in some of the earlier robberies but was as surprised as everyone else that the stable where he worked had become a target. Joseph Rose must have been teasing information from him over weeks until he knew all that he thought was necessary to send his three stooges on yet another mission. It seemed clear to me that Dan had played no part in that robbery.

The one thing the thieves didn't know was that all Mr. Butler's horses were branded under the tail. When he found out, Joseph Rose refused to touch them. Less wary, Browne and Green had attempted to sell the beasts and found themselves arrested for horse-stealing. Hoping for a favourable sentence, they had admitted to a host of similar crimes, but fortunately had kept quiet about their fellow conspirators. On occasions, there was still a certain honour among thieves.

Mr. Brasier was rightly disappointed with the young man whom he had helped, only to find his kindness thrown back in his face. He felt enough was enough, but was still unprepared to throw the boy, as he still was, on to the streets. So he had arranged an alternative path for him to follow.

Another distant member of the Brasier family was a sailmaker in Harwich, far enough away to make it a fresh start. Mr. Brasier had dug into his own purse to fund an apprenticeship for Dan Malden. He was still only seventeen, and though older than many apprentices start, he was sharp enough of intellect and nimble enough of hand to suggest he would soon make up for lost time.

I listened to all this and much more that he had to tell me. Why, I wondered was he there. It had to be more than simply to recount the information he had just imparted. I was right. There was a corollary to all this.

By all accounts, though it had not been his choice - he had been offered no choice - Dan had settled in Harwich and begun to learn his trade. There would never be a shortage of demand for sailcloth on the East coast; it was a decision not without merit. Unbeknown to him presumably, word had reached Thomas Brasier that the three Norfolk horse-thieves had been arrested somewhere near Diss and were set to appear at the Thetford Assize the following week. It was a grim suggestion that was made to me that evening, but one that deserved my support if I wanted to help Dan make his way in the world.

By road, from Ipswich to Harwich in winter can be as much as thirty miles. The shorter routes involve roads that by early spring are impassable unless still frozen hard. It was a wet March. By contrast, by boat, with the tide right and a favourable wind, the journey can be as little as two hours. So it was I found myself transported the next day aboard a wherry to the port of Harwich to seek out the sailmaker in question. I carried with me a letter from Thomas Brasier. It was an uncomfortable journey. What began as a rainstorm became a thunderstorm and the electric fluid flashed across the estuary. I was terrified. The story was still told how twenty years earlier four had been struck and killed in such a storm on that patch of river. But I arrived at Harwich none the worse apart from a soaking.

Dan was intrigued. I claimed I knew less than I did and with him caught the incoming tide back to Ipswich. From there, two coaches took us first to Diss, then on to Thetford, where we afforded ourselves the most basic of lodging. All the while, Dan believed we were attending the fair at the end of the Assize week to view a horse, which might be worth Dan's former master purchasing. I was glad to be with Dan again. The weeks had not passed easily in his absence, and though I had lacked neither work nor company, there had been something between us that I was only too glad to rekindle. Dan was more comfortable with me than he had been for a while. I only hoped that the deception he was about to discover would not turn him against me again.

Much of the town was given over to the fair that Saturday morning and there were many entertainments. Leaving our lodgings, we joined the swelling throng. Standing proud at one corner of the market square and close to the courtroom stood the gallows. Specially erected to accommodate two capital offenders, it was a grim reminder of the dangers of a life of crime. We found ourselves surrounded on all sides by a growing body of men, women and children. From quite nearby I could hear the bellman tolling the cart carrying 'Jack Ketch's victims'. It came closer and passed quite near to where we were standing. As Dan looked at the two chained aboard that cart, the colour drained from his face. He recognised them. They were none other than Abraham Browne and Robert Green. I learned later, that the third man, John Smith had been reprieved, which was hardly a reprieve as it meant a life spent in slavery on a Virginia plantation. But at least he had kept his life. Browne and Green were about to lose theirs. I honestly believed that it was the first hanging that Dan Malden had ever witnessed. At Ipswich, such events were carried out well beyond the town, up on the heath. Here, it was in full view of anyone caught up in the day's diversions. This was the impression that Thomas Brasier had intended to create - the full horror of a public hanging, made all the more horrific as Dan had only recently sat and drunk and planned thefts with the two about to die.

He pulled his old green jockey cap down over his head, almost afraid that the two on the scaffold would identify him. Then came the dreadful ceremony of it. The priest, reciting his verses, the warrant authorising the punishment, and finally, the statement by the men themselves, confessing their guilt and beseeching the crowd to acknowledge the justness of their fate and to refrain from like wickednesses themselves.

It was a short drop and it was not a quick end that was met by either man. Browne writhed and twitched for some minutes. Green seemed to slowly choke. They hung there for some time before their bodies were removed. At least it had not been decided to gibbet them. I think that was more than Dan could have taken.

We returned in silence, by way of Bury on the following Monday. Sunday travelling was frowned upon at that time. Dan went back over the water to his sail-making and I, having promised to meet with him quite soon, went home. It was odd; there was a closeness of spirit there, but now also a distance created by events shared. Thomas Brasier was well satisfied that his lesson had been learned. I was not too sure.

Chapter 7
The words of Dan Malden ~ 1729 & 1730

The more I thought about it, the angrier I felt. Now it was not just my grandfather, Tom Brasier, manipulating my life, but Mudge as well. I was seventeen; I had proved myself as a jockey; I had a wife, or as good as; I was even prepared to go along with what appeared to me little more than a version of slavery for the benefit of others - It was not for mine, that was certain. I had no intention of working in a sailmaker's shop for the rest of my days. It just seemed to me that wherever I went and whatever I did in my life was at the behest of others. I had realised all too quickly that my visit to Thetford had nothing to do with horses. They'd already made it clear enough that I'd be lucky to get within a country mile of a thoroughbred in the future. Sad that! I still wore my green jockey's cap, just to let the folks in Harwich know that whilst I might have hit low times, I had once amounted to something and would again.

No, first it had been my parents, then my grandfather, now my master. It was like I was a child all over again. So like a child, I had to be shown what happens to bad boys. As if I didn't already know. I'd seen men hanged before - and women! As kids we all used to follow the cart up to the heath to watch them dance. In those days I was freer than I would ever be again. I just yearned for that kind of freedom.

I missed my friends, Joe and Mary. They didn't have to bow the knee to anyone. They travelled the roads, getting richer. I was temped, I'll tell you... to run off and join them, if I'd only known where to find them. But I didn't. Instead I looked out at the sea and at the boats coming and going, to and from places beyond my imagination.

When you go down to the docks in a town like Harwich, it makes you realise how many different trades are employed in the building and maintaining of a ship. Sawyers, carpenters, shipwrights, riggers, caulkers, blacksmiths, painters, and of course, sailmakers. And they are only a few of the army of workers necessary to build and prepare a ship for a seaward voyage. Then also, you have banks of clerks sat on tall stools working on chest-high sloping desks, dipping their quills into ink-encrusted inkwells, writing painstakingly, filling great ledgers with the business of a sea-port.

That was the thing that held me there: being able to look out on the sea and dream. There were few other comforts. Even the warmth of Mudge's body beside me was a treat I was rarely able to enjoy any more. And I was not used to spending my days indoors. I bitterly missed the open air, especially as spring came on: the rides along the foreshore; galloping on the heath; the excitement of the race. All gone - I know, to an extent it was my fault, but bad luck had befallen me as much as anything else and now I turned my eyes seawards.

The odd thing was I wanted to hate the sailmaker's shop, but somehow I didn't. I loved the smell of linen canvas freshly cut, the tar and turpentine smell of the hempen rope; the oil and beeswax and varnish and the host of scents I began to recognise and remember. And all I learned there would stand me in good stead for when I went to sea, as I knew I should.

I was not entirely restricted to Harwich. My master had teams working all along that part of the coast: at Ipswich, at Walton and at Brightlingsea. Ferries plied across the mouths of the Stour and the Orwell, and along the Essex coast. Sometimes there were deliveries to make or tools and materials to pick up, so, as I became more of an asset and less of a liability, I would get to visit my home or meet with Mudge. But our times together were fleeting and I knew she was seeing other men. If our parting had come suddenly, it might have proved more painful, but somehow we just slipped away from each other with no great hurt and no great sense of bitterness. Still, I wished I did not miss her so.

I was older starting than any of the other apprentices around the port, but I was quick enough and found I had an aptitude for the trade. My master was a good teacher and believed I would make a good sailmaker. I still looked seawards and held my peace until the time was right.

The first day I arrived, I began work on my ditty bag. Every apprentice had to make one to hold the tools of his trade. But it was more than that. It was a means to learn and practice many of the key parts of the craft. In the making of that small bag, you employed four different stitches; you worked eyelets, spliced rope and even made a lanyard with a Turk's head to work as a slider. In the construction of that bag you practised the techniques necessary for making, repairing and maintaining the sails that were so vital to all who sailed the seven seas.

The advantage of sailmaking over, for example, my father's trade is that the tools are few and inexpensive; simple and portable. There is the sailmaker's palm, a leather device that has to fit your hand perfectly to enable needles to be pushed through the stiffest sailcloth. The blisters I had to begin with! But gradually my hands hardened up and as I learned to use oil and water to soften the seaming palm, it became almost part of me. I learned always to protect needles and knives and bench hooks against rust. However late it was or however tired you felt at the end of the day, you always had to make time to oil and wrap the metal items.

There were fids and awls and seam pommels. There were shears for the cutting of course, but no apprentice would be allowed to do that without many years training behind him. The canvas was far too precious to allow any to go to waste. And to allow the fabric to stretch and give, it had to be cut with the pattern of the weave in the right direction. There were charts and tables, full of figures for the calculation of how much seam to leave for any kind of sail on any kind of ship. I enjoyed the mathematics of it all. I soon proved I could work things out much quicker than the other lads and, given time, some of the old hands.

Whether the sails being made were triangular or quadrilateral, I could work out the number of cloths to be stitched for any given width. I knew before long the number of yarns in different thicknesses of rope; I could calculate the number of holes and grommets needed on a sheet. Every perforation of a sail and every join is a potential weakness in extreme weather, so I learned to turn such points into features of strength. I knew if I were ever to achieve my dream of going to sea, I would want the supplier of the sails that carried me away to take the same trouble as I was taking.

To be a sailmaker, you had to understand rigging and though we did not rig ships ourselves, in order for the mechanics of furling, unfurling and jibing to be understood, our learning went beyond the mere construction of sails. All this meant that by the time I was ready to leave the yard, I was more use to a sea-captain than any other landlubber leaving harbour for the first time.

A young man seeing ships come and go daily starts to wonder about other places. I would ask myself where they were going and what they would see. Sailors would sit on the quay telling their tales, and though you knew better than to believe every word, the curiosity grew. Sometimes they would tell of strange beasts - the hog in armour or the pelican of the wilderness. Sometimes, they had about them a long coiled snake, a parrot or a monkey that had survived the return voyage from Lord knows where. Then you could see for yourself they were not all tall tales. So still my curiosity grew.

Long days working and no money meant little chance to quench my thirst; or other appetites for that matter. So when it was suggested I might sign aboard a barque bound for Gibraltar and Morocco, I believed here was a way to take charge of my life. Oh I knew it would annoy my grandfather, he having paid out for my apprenticeship. I didn't care. I wanted to feel the wind in my hair and to see distant lands. I would come back rich, I told myself, and unburden myself of the debt I owed him.

So it was, still wearing my jockey's cap and clutching my ditty bag, I left the sailmaker's shop in search of adventure and maybe fortune. If I had cared to notice, few if any of the sailors returning to Harwich seemed to have made much by way of their fortune, but I was still full of confidence and it was with a light and joyous heart, I took to sea for the first time.

There was a gentle breeze blowing that morning and the sails were filled with it. As soon as the stern rope was let go, the barque sailed steadily away from the pier and was soon leaving land. There was no-one to wave me goodbye or shed a tear. That was the way I wanted it to be.

It was a gentle introduction to the sea. We were worked hard but the elements were in our favour as we followed the coastline southwards. That night, sleep came easily. I found that by the time I turned into my hammock without removing my clothes, my head ached, my forehead burned and I was instantly overcome by my exhaustion, but awakened wholly refreshed.

That second day the wind increased and the vessel began to make more noise over the bows. The white foam began to rush past and the tops of the small seas splashed up against the prow, landing in spots upon the deck. Our ship was loaded: she did not lay over but was carried along in an upright position.

As the sea became rougher, she began to pitch; her ropes strained in every direction. The air seemed full of water. Sail after sail was taken in, but still we were driven, seemingly at the mercy of wind and tide. At that moment, not for the last time, I questioned why I had embarked on such a mission. The sailmaker's shop appealed more then than it ever had whilst I had worked there. I can tell you, from what I know now, I would sooner be a chimney-sweep's boy than remain a merchant seaman.

Feeling sick and turning away from a gusting gale was a permanent state during the first days of that voyage. And if you retreated below decks, you were met by the indescribably foul smell of bilge-water; enough to turn the stomach of even the most seasoned sea-dog.

As for my companions: they were the roughest assemblage

of salty scallywags, hardened seamen, wharf-rats, thrown together with former landsmen like myself. But enough of them knew their business well enough to ensure safety and a successful trip. When you share a few feet sleeping space with a dozen or more such characters, a comradeship develops. A ship's crew are a rough and a disparate lot, but all your lives depend on the skills of one another so there is a closeness among sailors that transcends any other I have known.

In many ways being on ship is like being in gaol, only the food is worse, the dangers greater, the discipline stronger and there are far worse criminals ploughing the seas than ever inhabited most prison cells.

There are long periods of inactivity. So men seek diversions, some creative; others less so. My first storm over, and only beginning to feel I belonged to my digestive system once again, the sun shone, a calm descended on us and our company idled their time away as sailors do. Men fished with lines trailed out behind the boat, carved bones, played on pipes and home-made fiddles, danced, skipped over ropes or sewed intricate designs on bags and kerchiefs.

And we talked. I spoke to one old sea-dog they all called Napper. He had a strange accent I could not identify. He had been in the Navy, sailing under Admiral Byng in the attack on Sicily. He had worked on colliers and slavers and whaling ships. There was nothing that man had not experienced, from being cast adrift by buccaneers to being shipwrecked on a Portuguese outpost in the South Seas. He even claimed he had known Benbow, but I looked at him and I had my doubts. Still, I looked forward to the times when I could return and regale my family and friends with such tales.

What became clear from such conversations was that any fortune I had hoped to make from my travels would not be easily made as a lowly seaman on a trading ship. Sometimes men jumped ship and made their way in foreign ports. But I spoke none of the languages of the places of the Mediterranean to which we were headed and it seemed that my most appropriate next step was to sign for His Majesty aboard a ship of war.

"It'll be a good time to be taking the bounty," said Napper. "We are in a period of peace and even the Spanish leave our shipping alone. It was not always so."

"Then why do we still have a Navy?" I asked.

"The French, the Dutch, the Spanish: they all look upon the English fleet with fear. The truth of the matter is a third of our ships are not even seaworthy and the sailors have become fat and lazy from inactivity."

It sounded an easier and a better paid regime than the one I was at that time employed in.

"But there is still the chance to come home a rich man. Our navy polices the seas, and buccaneers and privateers in the Barbadoes are finding their booty confiscated and shared amongst the naval crews."

It all sounded so good. Only later would I learn that nothing in life comes easily, and these were merely the ramblings of an old man who could always see the benefit of being employed elsewhere.

Sailing towards Gibraltar, we hit a sudden squall.

"Aloft and get it in," called our Captain, and as one, we were up and furling sails as the ship began to pitch into a cresting sea. These were dangerous times. Such charts as we had were of doubtful veracity. We were close to shore and though weights were put down to sound for depth, the rudder glanced off a sunken rock and we had to put in for repairs. We fell in with a Spanish brig and bought oranges and other refreshments.

It was there we had the misfortune to lose a man who fell from the main topsail yard and was dashed to pieces on the deck. It was a loss felt by all of our crew, for though he was a Romany fellow, we were only too well aware it could have been any one of us. He was buried ashore, in the sand at low water as he was known to be no Christian. Christians, I learned were buried above the high water mark and given a proper respectful service.

Our repairs made, our mission restarted, goods were traded. For a while our cargo holds were empty but soon began to refill and the ship rode lower in the water once more. We were tanned and I have never felt more healthy than I did in the days just before we embarked for home. 'Flying fish weather,' one old tar called it, though I had no reason to believe such things were anything but a fantasy on his part. It was glorious and we had the opportunity to roam the shops and markets of the ports of North Africa. I was able only to purchase a few items to take home with me. I had joined the company in a hurry and been unable to bring much money with me. A small advance was possible, but regarded as one of the lowest forms of life aboard, little by way of a loan was forthcoming.

I had already set my heart on taking up service aboard a naval ship just as soon as it was possible.

Our return would take us first to the Thames, before making back for Harwich. It was an uneventful voyage. Even Biscay was calm and we made the Lizard, from where we took a pilot off Dungeness before arriving at Gravesend. It was there I left the ship. I had no intention of returning to Harwich.

Chapter 8
The words of Daniel Malden Senior ~ 1730

My father-in-law, Tom Brasier, appeared at the door.

"Is Dan here?" he asked.

"No, we've not seen him for a month or more."

That was so. It was also unusual. Though I had not been close to my elder son for some time, he did make a point of visiting his mother on a fairly regular basis.

"Then it must be true."

And so he told us what he had heard. Telling only one of the other apprentices, Dan had disappeared taking little other than his jockey's cap and his ditty bag. The message was that he had gone to sea, and not to expect him back for some time.

Knowing how Mary would feel, I led Tom outside.

"Are you sure?"

"Well, no, that was why I came here."

"Have you tried Mudge?"

"Of course. She hardly seemed surprised."

I quite liked the woman he sometimes called his wife. She was a bit rough, like most of the females that frequent the harbour area, but there was a warmth about her you could take to. I also believed she was good for Dan. She gave a bit of stability to his life, and though they always seemed to be at odds with one another, there was clearly a strong attachment there on both sides.

I thought of how, in the early days of my marriage, I had stood on the dock wall and watched ships set sail for foreign lands and wondered what my life might have been if I had become an adventurer. I could remember too the day of Dan's birth when I had looked out across the Orwell and imagined this very thing.

Then I thought of how I was going to have to break the news to his mother and cursed him for his lack of consideration. Of course, it was in all probability a momentary decision. He wanted no goodbyes; no reason to reconsider; nobody to attempt to change his mind.

It had left Tom in an awkward situation. He was the one who had begged a favour from his cousin, speaking of Dan in glowing terms. He had paid for an apprenticeship that would almost certainly never be completed. I made my peace with him, then went to break the news to Mary.

She, of course, thought the worst. So many ships never returned, or merchant seamen signed aboard naval ships and went to fight, facing far greater dangers. I tried to tell her that her son - our son - was a survivor, but I couldn't put her mind at rest and having related all the reasons why this was all our fault, she cried herself to sleep. She slept more than I did. I lay long hours awake wondering what he had taken on. I had helped fit out ships but I had no great knowledge of life aboard. A ship to me was a means of transporting people and goods as quickly as possible from one piece of dry land to another. It was not my way of life and I had long ceased to envy those that lived it.

Though enquiries were made, it was hard to be clear exactly which ship he had sailed away on. It seemed likely he had signed aboard a brig bound for Gibraltar and North Africa, but where its voyage would ultimately lead, no-one was very sure. From time to time, people would come calling in search of Dan. Mudge, I heard, had moved in with a ferryman and showed no knowledge of and little interest in our son's whereabouts. Then, first one disreputable character would turn up, then another.

My niece, Mary Brasier was one of those. She came twice that year, once with a man my wife recognised: Joseph Rose. I noticed he had been branded on the hand as a thief. He had been to the tattooist to have the letter 'F' for felon changed to look like a mermaid, but I could tell. My niece was certainly a pretty girl and she was dressed smartly. But I still wouldn't have trusted her any more than I did when she was a small child. I was glad to be able to tell her truthfully that Dan wasn't there and we had no idea of his whereabouts other than that he was at sea.

The second time she came, she had two other men in tow. At the time their names meant nothing to me. It was only later we would all learn the names of the Gregory gang as their exploits filled the Ipswich and Bury newspapers and were on everybody's lips.

Highwaymen were the scourge of the time and though the crime still occurs today, then it seemed to be far worse. Most who travelled any distance then were wealthy; many carried their wealth with them. Though there were occasional successes on the part of the authorities, all too often the worst outrages imaginable went unpunished. The roads out of London were regular targets, especially once you got out into the countryside. There must have been territories occupied by certain gangs and individuals. As one group of criminals was brought to justice, another took its place; often proving more violent and intrepid than the last. No sooner had they executed the Blake brothers, than the likes of Rowden, Gregory and Turpin began their depredations.

There were those who looked upon them as heroes, symbols of the poor man's fight against the power of the rich. But I met them, several of them, and I can tell you, they made my blood run cold. There was little by way of decency or humanity about any of them. And I was certainly glad to tell them that my son Dan was not available to join them.

It was later in the year that a message came. It was the first indication Mary and I received that told us he was still alive. A sailor, newly docked at Ipswich, complete with tarred pigtail arrived at our door. He had been at Gravesend, near the mouth of the Thames and had been asked by a young man there to present himself to Mr. Daniel Malden senior, joiner of Ipswich. There were a lot of tears shed that day. It was not much of a message but at least he had returned safely. There was no indication that he was coming home, and in all likelihood would be signing aboard another ship just as soon as his money ran out.

We gave the man a meal and wished him well. He told us he would not be returning to the Thames so there was no point in sending a reply with him. The last I heard that sailor was bound for Hull.

I was tempted to leave my work and go in search of my son. That was what his mother wanted me to do, but it would have been futile. I did not know the area where he was living and anyway, I would probably have arrived to find him departed. Besides, I had four other children and as much work as I could manage. No, Dan was a grown man and had chosen his own way in the world. He always chose his own way in the world. And it was a way that continued to take him further away from his family.

Chapter 9
The words of Midshipman Andrew Carter
~ 1731 & 1732

It has never been easy to find recruits for His Majesty's Navy. Though we exaggerate the returns and underplay the demands, even in times of peace, the young men we entice into the service disappear as fast as we train them. Recruiting has tended to work in two ways. There were those we 'persuaded' to join the navy. What we used to call a 'crimp' would select a seasoned sailor and drink with him, matching him round for round until his money was exhausted and he was keen to borrow. Men like that didn't need to be pressed as such, but when they discovered their evening out had left them in debt to His Majesty, it was too late of course.

Lads like Dan Malden didn't need that treatment. They may have been a bit short on seagoing experience, but they soon learn, and he was certainly keen enough. He came looking for us. He'd only made one voyage at the time, but at least he knew a bit about repairing sails. He had his ditty bag over his shoulder as I recall. He wasn't very big, even though by that age he must have been full-grown. The Captain was reluctant to take him. In time of war they are less fussy, but we'd not fired a shot in anger for a year or more. Still, there was talk of making up ships' companies with prisoners sentenced to transportation. The Captain wasn't having any of that, although we needed to complete our crew fast. So we took him, and one or two others like him. He had come across from Gravesend to Chatham, where we were having a minor refit before service in the West Indies. He was one of a number of new recruits in my charge; most were instantly forgettable. I don't think it was only his later notoriety that made me remember him. No, I recall his part in that venture for a number of reasons.

"I will tell you about this ship." I spoke to all of them. "She was built in 1719 and is a sixth rate vessel of three hundred and seventy-five tons burthen. One hundred and six feet in length, she carries twenty guns and seventy men."

Facts and figures. Most were disinterested, but Dan Malden kept asking questions.

"How many vessels will travel with us," he asked. "Where precisely are we bound and what might we see when we get there?" He even wanted to know the purpose of our voyage. Some of this information I didn't know at that time, so I told him to be patient and he would find out soon enough.

Part of the refit involved new uniforms, and very smart they were too. The ordinary able seamen wore chequered shirts with long striped ticken waistcoats, buttoned down with black buttons. They had kersey breeches, hose and shoes supplied at the expense of His Majesty. Woe betide those who let it spoil regardless of the tasks they might have to undertake. We used to joke and say that any man receiving a bullet hole would have to stop and sew it up before resuming battle.

Gradually we became aware of our purpose. Ours was a small ship by comparison with many, but we were sailing one of four small gunships that along with two sloops of war were being sent to the West Indies to protect British trade interests from pirates, both English and Spanish.

"Mister Carter!" That was the Captain. "Running gear, Mister Carter, running gear."

We had barely left port and it was time to put every man to work. During the process of setting sail, all halliards, buntlines, clew-lines, tacks and sheets were thrown off the pins, so by the time the ship was underway, the deck was a welter of running gear. One of the first tasks was to coil down the loose ends until everything was shipshape and blackwall fashion.

After that there were many tasks to fill the long days afloat. There was swaying off the topsails, gangs of men pulling stays in time to old shanties. Dan Malden as I recall was small and agile;

ideal for slushing the lines. This meant he would be sent up with a mixture of tallow and galley-fat to wipe the lines to the larger sails to make them run more easily. It was a dangerous task as your hands became greasy and you could easily lose your grip.

As the days stretched into weeks, we all found it hard to cope with the food. The best you could expect was hunks of meat out of a harness cask, saturated with brine and foul-smelling grease. It was worse for the basic seamen than for the officers but even that was bad enough. The cook did his best. He was an amputee - he had lost an arm in some battle in days gone by so he couldn't climb the rigging any more. That was how he came to occupy the galley. He wasn't much of a cook, but there was no other work on a naval vessel for a man like that.

The soft wind days seemed interminable and we even at one point considered bringing out the oars. With smaller vessels such as ours, it was possible to haul back the guns and run oars through the sweep ports on the lower deck. But our men were no rowers and it would have gained us little, so much of the time, they idled their days away smoking clay pipes, tattooing one another or playing at dice or cards.

Inevitably there will be disagreements from time to time. Though we watered the rum and brandy, crewmen would save their ration until there was enough to make them drunk. Then real problems could arise. Discipline could be harsh. Sleeping on watch could mean a dozen lashes. Naked lights in the passages below decks were dangerous and commanded the same punishment. But most floggings were for fighting, not that it was ever easy to determine the true cause. On that voyage, I saw a man flogged for passing water on the gun deck during practice.

The Captain was a stickler for cleanliness, you see. He'd have teams of men holystoning the decks till they were so clean you hardly dared set foot on them. Blocks of sandstone dragged over brine, together with the bleaching of the sun would turn the wood white. That was how the Captain liked it, and there was plenty of time to spare.

Then just as we were beginning to wonder if we would ever make progress, after two months' baffling winds, we picked up the North-East Trades which we used to our advantage, finally sighting land off Antigua.

To begin with, the six ships of our little convoy remained together, but the intention was to separate, and attempt to lure out some of the pirates that had been troubling that area for some time. We looked innocuous enough, but our fire-power was greater than it appeared and we expected to achieve success. Most pirates at the time used small armed sloops, relying on their local knowledge and manoeuvrability to give them an advantage. In the past it had been the Spanish who had suffered the worst of their attacks but now the British had established large sugar plantations in the area, the valuables ferried across the ocean between the settlers and their families at home were at threat. A few of the buccaneers sailed larger vessels with greater numbers of heavier guns, but they were notoriously undermanned, and as it takes three men to man even the smallest guns, they looked more fearsome than they really were. That was how the Captain put it to us anyway.

"Take a sounding." That was the call the first morning after our arrival. Anchored offshore and beset by sea-mist, we had to know the depth we were sailing, so a line with a weight was put down. The weight was covered with tallow so you could see when you pulled it up whether the sea-bed was of sand or coral or rock.

We were anxious to get away, but that only became safe as the mist cleared and we gained more knowledge of the channel we were in.

Our patrol took us south towards Barbados and St. Vincent. Skies remained clear, which was not necessarily to our advantage. Ours was obviously a naval vessel, and pirate ships sheltering in the many hidden bays had no real need to engage with us.

But maybe it was the prospect of an easy victory and the opportunity to replenish their stores by stealing ours that brought out one of the worst pirates of his day; Roger Newbourne. We had traded stories over the previous weeks of the most famous names, most of whom had met their end at the end of a rope... Captain Kidd and Blackbeard, Calico Jack and Stede Bonnet.

We came upon one another so quickly there was barely time to load the guns, and after a single salvo we drew alongside for the boarding of her. We had broken out the arms by then and showed ourselves to possess such strength as to easily overwhelm Newbourne and his pathetic bunch. We took few casualties - Newbourne being struck twice early on in the melee that ensued. After that, sword and shot soon reduced his men to a quivering disarray. For them there would be no return to England to face trial. No, they would hang close to the scene of their atrocities. In the meantime, heavy irons would hold them, something that was quickly achieved.

It was time to examine their ship to see what booty they were carrying. Dan Malden and Jack Lord were detailed to search a section of the ship, under my instruction. These pirates may have proved easy prey for us but they had certainly been busy. We found two quarter-deck guns and a swivel gun, no doubt taken from their last victims. As well as a quantity of gold, there were munitions - pistols and gunpowder, stores of all kinds and, to our surprise, seven black slaves.

There is an unwritten law governing the retrieval of booty. Of course, by rights everything belongs to the Crown. But to enforce rigidly such a dictate would be unworkable and the retaining of certain 'souvenirs' by seamen was something one turned a blind eye to. Naturally, items with real inherent value were not accepted as a part of this practice. It was only fair. A small party such as ours could have made ourselves very wealthy, whilst others detailed elsewhere would have got nothing. No, most of the gains were sacked up and taken aboard for the Captain's inspection. All of the men could expect a small bounty at the end of the tour of duty. It was better that way. Otherwise jealousy could ensue and discipline would deteriorate. I like to believe that a remarkable degree of trust existed amongst our seamen, rogues though many of them were. At that time, any man aboard a ship of war could leave his valuables below without fear of being robbed by those serving with him.

I did notice the pocketing of trinkets and kept an eye open for any man who might over-reach himself in the interpretation of the practice of souvenir gathering. A brooch here, a knife there: all that was acceptable; even expected. Limits were set.

"Able seaman, that jewellery is to be surrendered, and well you know it!" A warning was necessary from time to time.

I did see Dan Malden pick up a box and open it. Closeted in velvet was a pair of duelling pistols - flint-lock and ornately carved. I gave him a glance and he closed the box. They were not for the likes of him: he was only too aware of the fact. But I did see him secrete a lesser weapon inside his jerkin and deliberated before deciding to let it pass.

By such means did that man come by a weapon, which I later learned he would put to an unlawful purpose. I never felt a shred of guilt over that. We trained men to use such weapons and doubtless he would have come by another pistol if not that one. No, so many of the seamen in whose hands we invested the needs of a nation were rough disreputable characters. Whilst they were at sea in the service of His Majesty they were being put to good use, and at least delayed the day when they might end up swelling the country's gaols; or worse.

Satisfied we had located the most valuable items aboard the pirate vessel, we ferried them over to our own ship, before a handful of us were left to sail the captured craft to the nearest friendly harbour. It was a nervous time for all. With less than a skeleton crew, had a serious storm blown up, as they tend to do in those climes, we would have been at its mercy.

As fate would have it, matters were bad enough. We made an offing in the lee of some islands but took on a firmer blow.

"Come, my lads, let us take in our small sails before night," I called in the hope it would be enough, but as our shrouds stretched out, still more furling was required.

I remember feeling the ship lurch and heel over, but

judicious use of the pumps and a competent steersman righted her before she could lay down.

"Are we to die together here?" asked the youngest of our little company.

"Not so long as you are with me," I remember Dan Malden say. "I was not born to drown unremembered in this forgotten corner of nowhere."

I grinned, but he said it with such passion, and sounded so convinced of the fact, it put the lad's mind at ease, and he was able to play a full part in the exercise. It could so easily have gone horribly wrong, but fortune was with us that day and we saw the vessel home without further mishap.

That was the most significant moment of an otherwise uneventful tour. There were minor skirmishes, but our greatest enemy was boredom as the months slipped away and we found ourselves heading for home.

I remember speaking to Dan Malden as we neared the Scillies.

"Will you be signing aboard for another tour of duty?" I asked.

"I may, but not right away," he replied. "I have old friends to find and with my pay, I may equip myself for the future."

I did not press him as to what his future might be. He seemed a pleasant enough young man and I guessed he would find service with a grand family somewhere. I knew nothing of his links with Gregory and Rowden and the man Turpin at that time, otherwise I might have tried to steer him back toward a life at sea.

The last I recall of him was seeing him walking away from the dock, his jockey's cap on his head and his ditty bag hanging from his shoulder. Unlike his compatriots, he was not heading for the bars and the whores of Chatham, but out towards the London Road and beyond.

Chapter 10
The words of Joseph Rose ~ 1733

There are a thousand ways of making money in this country, and most of them are against the law. Not that that was ever a problem as far as I saw it. But two visits to Chelmsford Gaol and one spell in Newgate had made me cautious, and my colleagues and I saw no reason to trouble the authorities any more than was strictly necessary, if you see what I mean. When I chanced to meet Dan Malden again in the summer of thirty-three, it was clear he was ready for action and in need of money in his purse. I hardly recognised him at first. Dressed in all the finery he could afford, but still looking like a tar who had just cut his pigtail off, he found Mary and me supping, as usual at the Black Horse Inn in the Westminster Broadway. He had been looking for us.

"Cousin!" he called as he caught sight of Mary. They hugged and he came on over. I ordered him a drink of rum. I knew he had been at sea and assumed that would suit him. But he ordered a jug of ale and then proceeded to down both, as if he were making up for lost time.

"We came to visit you - three times," Mary said. It was true. I was never too sure Dan was really cut out to join our way of life, but Mary had this thing about family, and was of a mind to include him as and when he was ready.

"Where have you been all this time - and you looking so elegant and all?"

"I've been to the West Indies and to Gibraltar and such places as you could only dream about," he replied.

"And come back a rich man, so it seems. So what would you be doing with the likes of us?" I asked.

"I made my way for a while and since I came ashore, I've been home to settle my affairs there," he told us. "I intended to make matters right with my grandfather... our grandfather," he said, looking at Mary. "Now after taking my ease a bit, I find that I could do with a little more means than I have access to at present. I may look well to do, but it cost me all I had left to make it that way. Our meetings before have always proved profitable, and so I hoped they might again."

As I looked at him, I couldn't help but smile. Even at twenty or so, he looked no more than a boy. I thought of the ruffians that were my usual company then, and wondered what they would make of him. With his unmarked skin and his healthy complexion he was a far cry from the likes of our merry crew. I pictured Jones and Walker and Rowden and Turpin with their pock-marked faces and evil glares. By comparison, Dan Malden seemed innocent and untouched by the world. He was hardly any younger than the Gregory boys, but they had a lifetime of criminal experience packed into their few years.

Still, looking the way he did had its advantages. He looked trustworthy, which, when you are trying to part a man from his money can prove a useful asset. Also I knew he could ride and, as he had been in the Navy, I guessed he could fire a pistol or wield a sword of some sort. I didn't know then that he had taken to carrying a weapon about him wherever he went.

Of the many criminal ways to make money, some carry greater risks than others. I had seen too many friends dangling at the end of a rope to be careless about my arrangements. Where crime is concerned, the likely return has got to outweigh the danger. That is the way I see it.

So, we met at the sign of the Black Horse. We knew it was safe. John Bowler, the landlord, would be deaf to anything he heard and soon let us know if anyone came calling who was too curious about our business. That was why it had taken Dan so long to find us. He had followed a trail across the East End of London before a drink or two had loosened the lips of a lad named John Wheeler. When I learned this, I determined to put Wheeler right about his carelessness. Careless it was, as he had no knowledge that Dan Malden was truly a friend. The next time might spell danger.

At that time, our fraternity was involved in all manner of lucrative business. There were large houses aplenty around the outer parts of London. But it was necessary to know where people were armed and where you might be recognised. It helped to go disguised, although you knew if you did it was a hanging offence should you be caught. But then so was stealing enough to make it worthwhile, so I don't see it made a whole lot of difference.

The highways were always a fruitful source of money and valuables. You would be amazed to know what travellers carry about their person purely because they can't trust their own light-fingered servants if they leave the stuff at home. But you can't just set yourself up robbing travellers anywhere. Each man has his patch, you see... until he gets caught and then usually someone else moves in. When they hanged George Scroggs in July of thirty-two, several of us had it in mind to fill his shoes, but at Enfield and Edmonton, they collected for a bounty to place on the head of any man fool enough to rob travellers on the highways there. That's when we knew to leave well alone and head for Barnes Common or Epping instead.

Then there was coining - casting false coins is easier than you would realise, but the utmost care must be taken in passing them. It is never wise for common folk such as us to appear to have too much money about their persons. It is like a poor man attempting to sell a rich man's horse. It lays you wide open to arrest and all that that might bring.

Next, there is prostitution. In London there is every kind of vice on offer that you like to mention. The practitioners range from the fine ladies of Covent Garden to the pox-ridden whores of Whitechapel. But they all need their pimps and protectors. That's where we come in. Though Mary never walked the streets herself, she knows how to recruit young girls. Enough young lasses turn up lost and broke and starving, and looking for a way to put bread on the table. They may not all be great beauties, but even a poxy face can be covered with make-up, just so long as a girl is willing to offer a man a good time.

Street crime was rife, but we generally left that to the kids. There were too many constables on the look-out for pick-pockets and distraction thieves. The youngsters used to work in pairs - a pretty girl to lure the man's eyes away from his valuables and a young man to, in one movement, brush up against him and filch his pocket-watch. It was a risky business. At one court session in 1732, they hanged nine and cast thirty for transportation, and all under twenty years of age.

Which was why we used to meet in one of a handful of drinking houses to plan for making the greatest profit from the lowest risk. And it was one such plan that would include Dan Malden.

"What brought you back to London? I would have thought after all this time you and that woman of yours would have had a few things to do together." Mary was fishing - keen to know the latest news.

"You mean Mudge - she's shacked up with some sailor. I don't need her. Not no more I don't"

So that was it. You could see the suffering in his eyes. As if he had expected to walk back into her life and pick up again just because for once he had a bit of money in his pocket. Without her there was no need for him to stay in Ipswich. I sensed his pain. For all that, it made me wary. He felt abandoned and unloved. Men with nothing to live for are apt to take risks that the rest of us wouldn't. It made me uneasy.

Another man joined us that afternoon - an Irish tinker by the name of John Murphey. Like most of his kind, he was known by a host of names - I heard him called Bourk and O'Brien and O'Flaherty to name but a few. He had worked with us before, finding and setting up targets for burglary. This time he had found a large house, ripe for the picking.

"It's a little beyond Lewisham, south of the river, in Kent,"

91

he explained, just as soon as I'd introduced him to Dan and explained he was one of us and could be trusted.

"We'll have to hire horses then," I said, "It'll need to be worth our while."

"That it is," Murphey replied, "It's the home of a Thomas Venables. He has a carpentry business and has done well with it to such an extent that the house is full of good things. But there is more."

"There will need to be if we are to go as far as Lewisham," I told him.

"Listen up and I'll tell you. The man is working on a large commission. I have a friend who is going to let me know when the money has been payed over. If we time it right, there should be a small fortune in that house."

"But when will that be?"

"Before Christmastide."

"But that is months away. And what are we to live on in the meantime?" Good idea or not, it was far too distant.

"There is always Finchley Common and the rich fools that cross it."

"True, but even that is safer when the nights begin to darken."

"Then we shall just have to rely on the fair ladies to keep us in food and vittles."

And with that, we downed our drinks, and dismissed such things with a laugh, hopeful that other prizes might soon fall our way.

Dan had nowhere to stay, so for the next few weeks, he lodged with Mary and me. We had a couple of upper rooms at the rear of a place in Dawes Street, not far from the Black Horse, which was our favourite haunt at the time.

We gradually introduced him to our ways of working and to be honest, he fitted in better than I expected. He was good with the girls. The younger ones trusted him and the older ones mothered him. All in all, he didn't go short of company though

Mary was convinced he missed the one he'd left behind in Suffolk.

Eventually he moved out and settled in with Polly Buckley, one of the girls in his charge. I can remember when we first found her. She was unsure of her age, but could not have been more than fifteen. For all that she was an experienced bawd, having been debauched by her mother's lover in Ireland where she formerly lived. She came in search of work, but we needed to pay for her to be given the mercury treatment as she carried an infection, and we take a pride in the health of the girls we have to offer. The medication made her very moist in the mouth and she tended to drool, but she was a pretty enough child and popular with the gentlemen. She had a particular fondness for Dan Malden. He moved in with her; he said better to protect her, but to my way of thinking she was better equipped to protect herself.

They kept a good measure of company together, but so long as she continued to work the streets, I had no reason to complain. It could hardly have been a love match as he continued to send letters to the Suffolk woman... 'Mudge', I think he called her. I know that to be so, as Mary often helped him in the writing of those letters. His penmanship was not so good as hers. She told me his letters were full of passion and no mention was made of his relationship with Polly Buckley.

It must have been around the middle of October when the group of us met up at the Punch Bowl in Bloomsbury. It did not pay always to discuss our business in the same hostelries. This was another safe house and close to John Murphey's lodgings. Whilst Dan remained in London, Mary and I had been into Essex for a couple of weeks, trapping deer with the Gregory boys and Turpin; the one they called 'The Butcher.' He was a dour character if ever I saw one... tall, upright and broad at the shoulder, but thin of face, especially at the bottom. In a way, his tanned face sort of tapered away. He was an evil-looking character. They called him the Butcher and it wasn't only in recognition of his trade. No man would want to be on the wrong side of him.

Dan Malden had managed the girls in our absence. Now

we were back we had another plan to return to. John Murphey refreshed our minds regarding the carpenter from Lewisham.

"You know as how I told you this character, Venables, is expecting a payment for a large piece of work? Well, I have it on good authority that he will receive that money in exactly fourteen days and it will remain in the house for several days more. That is when we need to be ready to part him from it, and anything else that takes our eye while we are there." Murphey's voice almost sang the words and we sat entranced, Dan Malden, Mary Brasier and myself.

There was one other man there, older than the rest of us, but we had included him in our plans before. His name was Humphrey Walker... an irritating man in many ways, but he had his uses. He could work locks - better than that; if he couldn't open a door by gentle persuasion, then he had the strength of most men half his age and could usually force his way in.

"We shall need a horse apiece and no questions asked," I said. "And a pistol or two to put the fear of God in them."

It seemed that as far as we could tell, the old carpenter lived with his wife. There was an apprentice, bedded down in the workshop, but he was little more than a child and we did not anticipate having a great deal of trouble with him. Added to this, Venables' son-in-law lived in a separate building across the yard, but we surmised that if we were quiet enough, we would be out of there before anyone else knew we had been. Off and away we would ride, a whole lot richer than we had ridden there. That was how things were intended. The truth of the matter was to turn out entirely differently.

The night we had chosen should have been foggy. That would have worked to our advantage. As it was, after days of still misty weather, a storm broke and it was wild night indeed. The wind must have been blowing almost a hurricane. It was deathly dark, about one o'clock in the morning, when we rode from Lewisham to the far end of Sydenham Common. By way of a marker, we were looking for the sign of 'The World's End' beerhouse, but in the driving rain it was hard to see anything. Reaching what seemed to be the farthest house on the common, we dismounted and gathered together to light a lantern in the shelter of the yard. Murphey lit a candle and Mary used it to light the lamp. Some hot wax fell on his hand and Murphey cursed aloud.

"Keep your voice down," warned Walker. "Do you want them all awake before I have the door open?"

"They'll not hear us in this gale," Murphey called out. He was loud - recklessly loud and I guessed he had been supping from a flask on the way there. About then, the storm must have eased and the moon appeared, lighting us up as we stood there in the yard.

Suddenly, above us the casement moved open and a voice could be heard.

"Who are you and what do you want on a night such as this?" the voice asked.

Any thoughts of breaking in subtly and silently evaporated. Walker grabbed for a large sledge hammer that he had brought with him and began to belabour the door, calling out to the owner that if he did not co-operate, he would be murdered along with the rest of his household. We all joined in with equally threatening cries, pulling our hats down over our heads by way of disguise.

But the old man was not going to give in that easily. He fled up the stairs and he and his wife held their backs against the door, so as to impede our progress any further. Walker applied the sledge hammer to the wainscot beside the door and the wall began to give way. He struck the old man with the hammer, cutting his head. He would probably have finished him there and then, but the old fellow grabbed at the hammer and held on tight, calling out "Murder!" at the top of his voice.

Venables' wife grabbed hold of Mary, and I wrestled her to the ground, where she lay groaning. The next I remember, the apprentice and a maid appearing from an opposite landing, but Murphey held them at bay with a pitchfork he had conjured up from somewhere. Dan Malden held a pistol at arm's length. The apprentice attemped to dart by, and Walker jabbed at him with the pitchfork, but it was so chaotic that all he succeeded in doing was to jab Murphey in the stomach. The Irishman lay bleeding and clutching his wound. I don't think he was seriously hurt but he seemed to believe he was dying.

The fray went on so long, the old man's face and hands must have been nearly beaten to a pulp, but still he put up a mighty resistance. We must have completely forgotten about the noise we were making as a voice called out from the house across the yard. Murphey picked himself up, still clutching his stomach and went back downstairs to the yard where he yelled up to the face at the opposite window.

"If you durst come down here, we'll murder you like we'll murder any man that gets beween us and our booty!" he called.

If it was intended to sound threatening, it did not work. The son-in-law was upon him before he knew it and, armed with a poker, began to attack him. Then with the force of his blows, the poker flew from his hand. Murphey still had the sensibility to grab it and use it to his own advantage. By this time both men were covered in blood. Murphey got his assailant down and would probably have done the murder he threatened had not the carpenter's daughter appeared, in her shift, big with child. Picking up an iron rod, she began beating Murphey about the head, enabling her husband to get clear, upon which they both beat the Irishman until he lay senseless in a pool of his own blood.

In the moonlight, from the window I could see the young couple making for the nearest houses to raise the alarm. It was clear to me then that although we had not found what we had come for, it was time to leave and at least save ourselves.

"Come on," I called. "They will raise the town and we shall be taken."

We left a scene of devastation and serious wounding. In the yard we found Murphey unconscious and bleeding and carried him, with much difficulty towards where our horses were tethered.

The carpenter's daughter was there but I held her as the others mounted and slung our insensible colleague across a saddle.

"Shoot the bitch!" I called to Dan Malden, but soft of spirit, he put the pistol away inside his tunic. I suspect it had never even been loaded. I flung the woman down. She groaned before picking herself up and going off in search of her parents. I mounted my horse and we slipped away slowly into the night. The rain came on again and washed away most of our prints and our colleague's blood. But he was in a poor way and we knew he could not be conveyed much distance in that manner. We found a hut, unoccupied and offering a little comfort, and there we left him, intending to return to see to him when the day became light.

By that means did the rest of us return, empty-handed and missing one of our crew. It had been a disaster. It was easy to blame Murphey for being loud and uncontrolled; probably drunk. But none of us came out of that experience too well and we resolved soon after to leave houses alone and take to the roads.

We never did return for John Murphey, or whatever his real name was. Word was out that there was a hue and cry looking for 'a gang of desperadoes' who had left the scene of their latest crime leaving quite a collection of clues behind. We heard too that Murphey had been found, insensible and sorely hurt, and that if he recovered, he would be questioned and tried. To our relief, he never did. To be honest, there is not a lot of honour among thieves; not when they are out to save their own skins.

Chapter 11
The words of Mudge
(later to be known as Mary Malden) ~ 1733

I knew he had another woman. Don't ask me how I knew but I felt it, and I knew sure enough, just the same as I knew he didn't write those letters by himself. Not unless he'd learned a whole lot whilst he was away at sea. But I also knew he still loved me, and I him if I was honest with myself. But you can't fashion your life around a man like that. So in his absence I had settled in with an old flame who still held a passion for me - another sailor by the name of Harry Codd - I always had this thing about sailors.

When Dan came ashore and in search of me, I could smell the tar on him, and I was tempted, but it wouldn't have been any good - he'd have been off somewhere on some venture that didn't involve me. So I let him go. At the time I thought I might be carrying Harry's child, which limited my choices somewhat. But it didn't stop the tears falling as soon as Dan was out of my sight. And it didn't stop me yearning for his letters to arrive.

Of course, I was not expecting a child - not that time. I suppose you can say I was fortunate not to fall pregnant more often than I did. But it seemed there was something in my make-up that made it unlikely. When I was a whole lot younger, I fell twice; the first time when I was so innocent I didn't understand what caused it. But both died, both little girls, and though I was hardly careful after that, a mother was something I was never intended to be.

Mine was never an easy life and if I was honest with myself, I suppose I didn't really expect a lot of happiness. In a way, I didn't feel I even deserved it. But it had been good at times with Dan Malden and I had almost regarded myself as his wife at one point.

By the end of 1733, he had been in London for several months, but though I yearned for him, there was no way I intended to run off after him, only to discover he had a wife and child. Well, it seemed likely in spite of his loving letters.

Then, out of the blue, his father called. I'd not seen him for over a year. He was doing well in his business and we didn't really mix in the same circles, if you understand me. My man, Harry, wasn't there at the time. He wasn't at sea either. There was not much trade out of Ipswich that year and I was only too glad to get him out from under my feet. I'd found a coin or two and sent him round the dockside bars in search of work - any work - it looked like being a long hard winter.

"Good heavens, you're a stranger." He looked younger than I'd seen him, dressed in his finery. I understood Daniel Malden senior only troubled himself with the most expensive commissions and left the basic work to his two apprentices. I fussed around tidying up as best as I could, but my humble home still smelt like a dockside lodging.

"I came to see if you'd heard from Dan." He looked so very worried.

"Only the latest in a line of fairly similar letters."

It was true. I learned little about what he was really doing. As Mary Brazier helped him with his writing, she could keep a clear eye on what was being said. As a result, there was nothing about whatever activities he and Joseph Rose were involved in. I wanted to believe that he was safely employed in acceptable pursuits, but his letters lacked so much in substance, I had to be suspicious. There was also nothing in his writing relating to other women, but it didn't mean my fears were unfounded.

"It was just..." He stopped a moment. "It was just a coachman came in with an order for his master and he wondered if I knew..." Again he stopped.

"Go on"

"It seems the talk of Westminster that there have been these burglaries from houses close to London. And one went wrong. The gang responsible were routed, and one wounded so badly he has since died."

99

"I don't understand. What has this to do with Dan?"

"Word has it that some of the Essex gang were responsible and you know what that means?"

"Joseph Rose?"

"Exactly." He pulled a folded newspaper from inside his frock-coat. It was a copy of the Ipswich Gazette. I could read and write slowly, and was able to make out the report of a robbery at a house in Sydenham where one of the robbers had been mortally wounded. My initial fear was that it might have been Dan, but a later issue of the paper Mr. Malden also carried described the dead man as an Irishman by the name of Bourke, though it was said he had many aliases. I heaved a sigh of relief. But then the same thought crossed my mind as must have struck Dan's father.

All too often newspaper reports coming out of London were incorrect. Weeks later, they would announce that a previous description had been erroneous and needed alteration. So many of these criminals were known by a number of names. If they came to court, they wanted it to appear it was their first offence. Men didn't usually hang or face transportation for a first offence. How were we to know that this 'Irishman' was not a Suffolk man?

I felt sick and cold and helpless.

"Would you go and find out if he is safe?" Dan's father asked. "I'd be lost there. I'd be useless, and I still have a family to look after."

Why he thought I should be any more worldly than he, I have no idea. My first thought was, "How am I going to explain this to Harry?" But I knew in spite of everything, I had to go.

"I'll pay your return fare on the machine to London - an inside berth. And I'll see you have enough for your stay." I was grateful for that. I couldn't have done it on my own. I saw him to the door and started to make ready. At that time of year it was not a journey to undertake lightly. And knowing I would be searching for the kind of people that were the Essex gang filled me with apprehension.

In the end it would be a coincidence that would lead me to

him; in a way, a double coincidence.

Just a month or so earlier, I had helped a man who was hurt. Harry had found him collapsed beside the river at Wherstead Reach. With the help of a boat, he'd brought him up river and I was left to attend to him. To begin with, he didn't seem to have much of a chance. Someone had run a sword through him, neat as you like, under the collar-bone and out through the shoulder. He was well dressed, though dusty and mud-splattered, but there was money in his pocket - eight shillings as I remember. A large key hung on a thong around his neck. He had also a pistol thrust into his belt, recently fired by the smell of it. He kept mumbling about a horse, and later in the day, Harry came back with the animal he had clearly fallen from. You could tell from his hands he rode a good deal, as there were scars from constant use of the reins.

In the end he proved a lucky fellow as the sword had severed no main blood vessels and punctured no vital organs. He was weak from loss of blood and a fever held him for several days, but slowly he came back to us and we gradually teased his story from him.

In actual fact, again it was the Ipswich papers that gave us much of the story. Our patient, it seemed was a highwayman working the roads around Manningtree, between Ipswich and Harwich. On this occasion he had taken on a gentleman who proved too smart for him. With a loaded pistol he had accosted this doctor who lived over in the direction of Bury - MacGray I think his name was. He had held the pistol close to the man's breast, having first surprised him on the road and bid him deliver all he had on his person. The doctor had answered that as he had no haste to die he would give up a share of all he had and handed over the eight shillings we had found in the highwayman's purse.

Not satisfied with that, our man had attempted to search the doctor. This had been his undoing and a good example of why highwaymen work better in pairs. With the horse's bridle wound around his left arm and the pistol in his right, he was encumbered and this enabled the doctor to unsheathe the weapon he carried and to run the man through. The pistol went off, but missed the doctor and our man fell from his horse and was dragged away from the scene. At this, the doctor made his escape.

Wounded, bleeding and in great pain, the highwayman, with some difficulty remounted. But no sooner had he started off than he met another traveller who had heard the gunshot, so he pretended to be the victim of the attack and warned the other man to make haste as the road was not safe. He had told that man he was making for Colchester, then had taken himself off by a devious route in the other direction, finally arriving close to Ipswich before his strength gave out, which is when Harry had found him.

It was a mercy he did as no-one could have survived long in that condition without care and attention. I have tended to enough wounds in my time, so I was the right person to minister to our anonymous guest. Though there was a hue and cry out for the man who had threatened and robbed Doctor MacGray, no name was published and it was clear from the newspaper report that they expected their search to reveal a dead man rather than a living one.

I was intrigued by the key around his neck, but he never ventured to explain its purpose and I was reluctant to ask. He seemed grateful that I had not been too curious. Before he left us, ten days later, the man expressed his gratitude in two ways. He gave us a half share of the money he carried and, as he was heading for London, told us where he could be found should we ever need him.

He also told us the name by which he was known. It was 'Country Jack.'

Chapter 12
The words of Country Jack ~ Late 1733

There is cluster of buildings between Wapping and Whitechapel, just off Rosemary Lane, known as White's Yard. It is not exactly what you'd call luxury accommodation, but I had contacts there and it seemed a good place to lie low and recuperate. I still had a lot of pain in my shoulder, especially after riding for a day and a half, so I was glad to reach familiar ground.

You know you are nearly there when you pass the old church at Bow; then coming down the Mile End Road, there is the ducking pond on Whitechapel Green. With an effort of will you venture south toward the river. You can smell the Thames from some distance, even in the cold of winter. Open sewers run down to Limehouse reach. There are rats as big as dogs there and the stench is unbelievable. Providing the tide is in the right direction, it is all washed out to sea, but on a turning tide, it all backs up and can prove objectionable even to the grand folks living upriver from Westminster.

White's Yard lies close to the Ratcliffe Highway, and is commonly frequented by sailors looking for whores and entertainment. That disreputable place is little more than a filthy passage just north of the waterfront at Wapping. You can find girls from every country and every walk of life there. Flemish girls have set themselves up in numbers; many others are servants who lost their jobs for thieving or because their master made them pregnant. They all need the money for one reason or another, most because they have taken to the Geneva and can't lay off it.

Some say the Yard offers a better class of whore, and certainly some of the ships' officers tend to make their way there, but it is not a place to live by choice. As my name suggests, I am not a Londoner, nor would I ever wish to be one. But renewing old acquaintances is always pleasant and I felt in need of a little loving care. I knew where to find it. The Yard is an open court-yard surrounded by rambling tenements, some as high as four storeys. The Great Fire never reached that part of London, more's the pity, so most of the buildings are old and crumbling. Some are surprisingly recently built, but not with any skill or care, so they appear as damp and depressing as all the rest.

A large number of those living in that area are Irish. And there are a good few Jews. It is all too often assumed they are all rich businessmen and financiers, but most of them are as poor as the likes of us and live in squalor like the rest who occupy that part of London.

I was looking for a certain lady by the name of Ann Evans. She was well known in those parts as one to whom you could take all manner of goods and obtain a fair price. She and her sister-in-crime, Marcie Gray, were traders, so to speak. Gold watches, silk handkerchiefs, even the tassels off an altar cloth were their stock in trade. And on this occasion I had something to trade that wasn't even stolen.

It came hard, but I needed money and it would be some time before I could summon the strength to return to the road. I determined to sell my horse. It had taken all I had to settle my affairs in Ipswich; four shillings to Mudge and Harry who had nursed me, and another four for the stabling of my horse whilst I was fighting my way back to life.

So it was I arrived hungry and aching, hoping to strike the best of bargains to tide me over. I also needed accommodation and information as to where I might locate a number of old friends.

"Country Jack - well I never! I heard you were dead."

That was Annie Evans' first response on seeing me.

"I'm very pleased to prove to you I'm not, though I will admit I have felt better."

I must have looked in quite a state, as she found a blanket, wrapped it around me and put me straight to bed. I hardly remembered a thing until I woke the next day. It was practically noon, and Annie was on hand to offer me a bowl of soup, so hot it nearly burnt my throat.

"Here, let it cool a little. I know you must be hungry, but give it a moment."

But I was so keen to drink the soup, I was unaware of how it was scalding my mouth. I felt surprisingly refreshed. The ride had taken more out of me than I had realised. Then it occurred to me... my one asset... my horse...

"You'll be wanting to know about your horse. He's safe and in the care of a friend close by."

"I came because I need to sell him," I said. "And because I wanted to see you again." I remembered my manners just in time.

"He's a fine horse - stolen, I suppose."

"No, for once a purchase I made with my own money - well, not really my own money if I'm honest, but I did buy him; I didn't steal him. You'll find no other man's brand on him."

I was relieved to hear he was in good hands and it was agreed when I was fit enough, we would go together to find a buyer.

Suddenly remembering something else, I put my hand to my neck. Oh my God, it wasn't there! I panicked.

"If you're looking for that old key, I hung it on the back of the door over there, so don't you go and get yourself all worked up." And no more was said.

Annie's rooms included a cellar which housed a quantity of goods awaiting distribution. Some of it was her own; other items belonged to a network of thieves inhabiting that area. Over the next few days, I met a number of them.

Close at hand was a smith who gloried in the name of Clarence Germane. More amusing still was his wife, a large ebullient woman called Temperance, which was good for a laugh, as she was the least temperate woman I have ever met. She could outdrink the lot of us, and regularly did. We were close to the docks and there seemed no shortage of wines and spirits to augment the local ales.

Then there was another couple, John and Ann Holburt. They regularly supplied Annie with the proceeds of their night excursions. And there was Thomas George, a petty thief who called round from time to time.

As to the goods, much of it was stolen to order. Annie already knew where it was headed before it arrived. Sometimes traders would call with lists and go away with some of what they had come for, and a lot more besides. She was a good sales-woman was Annie. The least traceable items went to one of the Rag Fairs that had become a famous part of that area. One such fair was commonly found operating in Rosemary Lane, close to where I resided, but it was not there she meant to sell my horse.

Petticoat Lane lies on the boundary between the City of London and Middlesex. Consequently, the market that has sprung up there is in no man's land. The authorities of neither want to know about it, or to be responsible for regulating it. As a result, you can get anything at the Rag Fair there, not just clothing and fabrics. And you can sell anything there too. That was where Annie intended we should take my horse, the following Sunday.

"Most of the traders are Jews, and don't trade on a Saturday, their Sabbath. But no true Londoner minds a bargain so business is brisk on a Sunday."

It seemed Sunday trading laws just didn't apply in this little patch of no man's land. And as fate would have it, the pair of us set out to take my horse down there to sell.

I wasn't familiar with the place where he was being stabled. It was at the back of a bawdy house a few streets away in Well Close Square. It was a place I would become much more acquainted with; a beer-house called The Ship.

Annie was quite glad of the distraction and I was grateful for her company, for I knew the Rag Fair was not a place for out-of-towners like myself. You held on tight to your purse and you stayed focused on what you had come to do.

Shop-fronts spilled out into the street. There was a great profusion of people, animals and produce of all kinds. Clothes, in particular, were aplenty, and voices could be heard eagerly bartering.

"How much?" A man holds up a topcoat.

"Vun and sixpensch," comes the reply.

"Take one and twopence?"

"Ha!" the Jewish tailor cries, turning his back on the man.

But of course, that is far from the end of the transaction, and soon the two are in earnest discussion about prices and deals.

These tugs-of-wars of words were as much a part of the colour as the shops and the stalls themselves. As we moved along the street, we found stallholders and barrow-pushers offering their fish, their vegetables, their wigs and their hats. There were pawnbrokers and 'dolly-shops' lending money at exorbitant rates on items of little or no value at all to those with little chance of ever repaying it. And most pitiful of all were sellers purveying items which once had been beautiful, but now were just sad: silken dresses once worn by beautiful ladies, now fouled and stained; shoes formerly of the very height of fashion, but lacking soles and buckles; pieces of jewellery with broken catches and missing their stones. Anything could be found for sale there.

We did not need to remain there long. Prospective buyers found us and before I knew it, Annie was conducting what can only be described as an auction. Eventually, a gentleman she appeared to recognise offered what I felt was a fair figure and I found myself returning with a pocket full of coins, ranging from guineas to half-crowns. To my surprise, when I offered money to Annie for my keep, she refused it, saying that now I was fit I could put business her way. I was welcome to stay, she told me, seeing as I no longer had a means of transport. And so, for the time being, I did.

Another lady I came to know at that time was Elizabeth Shelton. She had rooms in Whitechapel, better than most, and she was introduced to me as someone who might put me in touch with those 'in the same trade' as myself. Her home was comfortable by the standards of the area. Others across the street and round the corner were far worse. I saw places where whole families lived in sodden cellars barely four feet high and with no natural light falling inside. Filth was piled in the streets around and disease stalked these places like the Grim Reaper.

It was not an easy time for the criminal fraternity in London. Parishes were combining to put constables out at any whisper of wrongdoing. Inhabitants even in our depressed area had made a contribution for an extraordinary team of Watchmen who walked their beat three or four times in an hour, day and night. Not that we expected to rob our own. No, we would always put at least two parishes between our homes and our indiscretions.

All crime was being treated as serious crime. Hangings were up, floggings too; and the pillory was never empty. Truly serious crime was punished with the full rigour and pageantry of the law. Crowds were drawn for such exhibitions like moths to a flame. And I was no different. Still familiarising myself with the area and its people, just before Christmas that year, I found myself following a crowd to Smithfield where an archaic form of punishment was being enacted.

A huge pyre had been constructed for the burning of two forgers, John Brown and Elizabeth Wright. Coining, as it was known involved no small measure of skill and a good deal of courage as I was to discover. The two were chained and dragged on sledges, crying and screaming as they went, before, nearly fainting with fear, they were tied back to back to a post and held as charges were read out. Then there was a brief moment of confusion as another document arrived. It was a reprieve of sorts for the man, who was to hang instead. Anxious to progress before any other alterations might be decided upon, a rope was thrown over a protruding spar and the fellow's writhing choking body hauled well clear of the ground. Every part of this must have been visible to the woman tied to the stake. Then attention moved to her. The fire was lit. Her bonds were loose enough to enable her to dance in agony as the flames consumed her and the crowds pushed dangerously forward to get a better view. Some took home pieces of the charred wood as souvenirs.

Unused to such savagery, I crept into an alley and was promptly sick.

Someone else was in that alley. She had crept there for the same purpose. To my amazement, it was someone I recognised. It was the woman from Ipswich who had looked after me. It was Mudge.

"Now what are you doing here?" I asked.

"Oh I'm so glad to find someone I know. London is so big and I don't know where to find him."

"To find who?"

"Dan Malden - You don't know him I suppose. He lives in London."

"I've never heard of him, but I'd have been surprised if I had - there's... thousands and thousands of people in London. But I do know a number of people and I can try to help you - It's the least I can do."

Then it occurred to me to ask, "Do you have anywhere to stay?"

"I'm at an inn not far from here, but it's too grand for the likes of me and I don't feel I'm mixing in the right company to locate Dan Malden."

She still looked white from the shock of what she had just witnessed. But gradually, her composure came back and remembering her mission, she asked, "I suppose you don't know Joseph Rose or any of the Essex gang?"

"I think most of the constables of England would like to find the Essex gang, and though I've heard of Joseph Rose, I have no knowledge of his whereabouts; but as I said, there are people where I am staying who might. However, I must warn you. These are dangerous people you are seeking and they almost certainly will not want to be found."

I didn't know then, but in helping her, as she had helped me, I was stepping into a whole new world of danger that carried every bit as much threat as my former life had.

As we made our way back East - it was a long way down Cheapside, having first retrieved her bag from the inn where she had been staying - I learned more of her desire to trace this Dan Malden. I was not over-hopeful but there were those I had met since my arrival that might be able to help.

My arrangements with Annie Evans had become a little more than a business partnership, so I felt it inappropriate to turn up there with what was, after all, a rather attractive woman. I chose instead to speak to Elizabeth Shelton regarding appropriate accommodation for my Ipswich friend. She was happy, she said, to find Mudge a room. Then there was the other matter.

"We are anxious to trace a certain Daniel Malden," I said. Elizabeth Shelton frowned.

"I can't say as that name means anything to me," she replied.

"He may be with members of the Essex gang," cried Mudge. "Joseph Rose or Mary Brasier."

"Look my dear, these are people who would not wish their names spoken of here, so keep your peace for the protection of all of us. As for your Daniel Malden, I honestly believe I have never heard that name before."

"You'd know him if you saw him," Mudge cried desperately, "He's small; shorter than you or I, looks little more than a boy but he may still carry the tar staining of a sailor on his head and he wears a jockey cap - or he did." She collapsed in tears, but I could see a change come over Elizabeth's face.

"Oh my God, it's Dan Morgan."

After a statement like that, there had to be an explanation. Following the Sydenham debacle, a number of the group had changed their names, separated and gone into hiding. By way of a further coincidence Dan and Polly Buckley had become 'Mr. and Mrs. Morgan' and set up home close by in Wapping. Dan had put his sailmaking training to good use whilst he waited for other more lucrative options to come his way.

Elizabeth took us both to the nearby Ship inn and she pressed her face up against the glass to see who might be inside. As her eyes became adjusted to the darkness of the tavern interior, she spotted what she was looking for.

"He's there, just round to the left, sitting in the corner," she reported. "You can go and speak to him if you like, but his woman is with him."

Mudge slunk round the door to obtain a clear view and convince herself this was indeed her former lover. It was dark and she took some time to get a good sighting. Satisfied, she returned outside unseen. Oddly, Mudge did not want to stay to meet him. It seemed to satisfy her to know he was alive and safe.

She left for Ipswich the next day without trying to arrange a meeting. For my part, I was intrigued. I have had to live by my wits since I was old enough to escape the clutches of my bitch of a mother and her brute of a lover. Nobody ever cared enough for me to leave their familiar surroundings and to go in search to find out if I was all right.

'What was so special about him?' I asked myself.

I decided I would take it upon myself to make the acquaintance of this young man, just as soon as it was possible.

Chapter 13
The words of John Holburt ~ Early 1734

His woman died that winter. She was a sickly kind of girl and had been prone to catching much that was in the air. Then she went into a decline until the little energy she possessed was no longer enough to support such a faint spark of life. It was as if she died of a lack of will to live, and Dan took it hard. Odd really! You could hardly say he ever loved the woman. He still sent her out whoring when she scarcely had the strength to stand.

But as I came to understand, she was the one thing that held him in London. Little else appealed - the noise, the filth, the smell, the poverty. He had never been truly accepted by Rowden and his cronies. He didn't have the physical presence to ride the road like Turpin and Gregory and Joseph Rose. They looked upon him more as a talisman, like the boy who carries the flag at the head of a regiment. And then, after the Sydenham debacle, when his lucky charm seemed to have deserted him, they made less and less contact. Following Polly's death, I am sure Dan Malden never felt more alone in his life.

That was when I came to know him. I forget whether he was Dan Malden or Morgan then. He may even have changed his name to Smith for all I know. We worked together for a while - yes, worked! Legitimately! I admit I too had sailed close to the wind for much of my life and working for a living was not my normal modus operandum. You may be able to tell from my way of expression, I am not an uneducated man. But an education and visible means of support do not necessarily go hand in hand. So even I had, on occasion, to sully my hands with physical labour.

It had been a wet and a windy winter. Trees and houses had been blown down in Moorfields; chimney stacks in St. James, resurrecting memories of the great storm of 1703. Ferry boats and others had been lost. The banks of the Thames had been breached in a number of places, especially upstream of Westminster.

Word was about that any men able to reach Richmond would find work rebuilding the terracing as far as Kew. At least a hundred men a day were required. I knew a friend with a boat and with a fair tide and a break in the weather, a number of us made our way there. It promised to be at least a month's work and good wages. There was mean and basic shelter for those hardy enough to take this on.

On the way upriver, as we took turns with the oars and holding the single sail into the wind, I found myself sitting beside Dan Malden. Though our lives had been somewhat different, we took to one another and by the time we made Richmond, were firm friends. I asked him what had drawn him to labour at such a wretched time of the year. It was then I learned about the girl Polly. I also learned that though the dead girl had left a gap in his life, it was not half as much of a gap as another woman back in Ipswich that he still hankered after.

"I have a problem," he explained. "My cousin Mary has moved away out of town and it was she who helped me to pen letters to Mudge. Now I have no-one with the necessary learning to aid me."

"Look no farther," I beseeched him. "Either I - or, if you prefer the advice of a woman, then my wife, Ann - will be at your disposal, just as soon as we have paper and quills to hand."

He seemed well pleased by that and over the rest of that week, as we worked together, he opened up to me. Each week ending, we came back to Wapping, either on the Saturday night or the Sunday morning, depending on the tide.

Slowly, as I gained his confidence, I learned more about Dan Malden - about his life as a jockey and at sea. Only very slowly did I learn about his criminal connections. As I have suggested, I have hardly led a blameless life myself, and though I might view my indiscretions as fairly minor in the order of things, the way our courts punish people seems now to take little account of that. It is by their way of thinking quite reasonable to impose the direst of punishments upon the least of offenders on the mere assumption that the offence for which criminals are being tried is probably only a sample of their total depredations.

We both had other reasons for seeking genuine employment. Talk was again of war, and the Press Gangs were out. We had seen them moving through Spittlefields and Shoreditch with drums, trumpets and hautboys. Bounties were being paid and men with known naval experience were being impressed into the fleet. It was not a good time to be found workless in the docklands of any great port.

At the same time, a move was afoot to clear the streets of unlicensed traders, vagabonds and street-walkers. It meant a temporary end to some of my schemes. I knew such a put-down was not sustainable, but needed to lie low, so to speak. We had worked much of the previous year, my wife and I, operating a gaming stall from a wheelbarrow. 'The Black Joke', we called it, and mighty successful it had proved until people grew wise to it. But there were always other games... However, the authorities were rounding up every woman with a barrow, and it was better to rest awhile.

So it was we made one another's acquaintance and by the time the King's birthday was celebrated on the first of March, we were of a mind to celebrate it together. Like most of London, it seemed, we took to the river that night and amid the ringing of bells and the firing of the great guns at the Tower, fireworks were played off from Cheapside that lit up the freezing night air. Sky rockets, wheel rockets and line rockets showered their sparks in a way that almost frightened the atmosphere. And we, true supporters of the King that we were that night, loved every minute of it.

Of course, monarchists are drawn from those that have, and at that time, we felt comfortably off - more than that; we felt that we had contributed to something that was great and important. Had we bothered to consider it at the time, we would have known our labours were purely of benefit to those with riverside estates in

Surrey, and our king was a German-born aristocrat with little concern for the majority of his people.

That was never more evident than when, a few weeks later, the Princess of Wales married the Prince of Orange. Already, our funds were shrinking, but like faithful subjects, we took ourselves off to St. James to join the assembled crowds to wave and to cheer.

"Did you ever see such a dress?" my wife said. "The train must have been ten yards long."

"They do say his suit was embroidered with real gold thread and that the buttons alone cost three hundred pounds apiece."

Somehow, details like that seemed obscene in the light of our own imminent poverty. Work had not been forthcoming since the river work at Kew. As for myself, I was not particularly sorry. Dan, for all his lack of size was far stronger than I, and had coped better with labouring long hours. Without his encouragement, I would probably have given up. After three weeks without work, he was as penniless as we were. The girls he used to run had drifted away. He had lost interest in pimping since Polly's death. But he was still open to other suggestions of a less than legal description.

The same names came up again and again at that time. We often met together, drank together. There was, as I recall, a fellow by the name of 'Country Jack.' I never did know his real name. He had been a highwayman and was 'resting' as we liked to call it, so we met him a few times, especially when drinking at the Ship in Well Close Square.

We had a common acquaintance - a woman called Ann Evans who could be relied to sell on anything of value that came our way. Shortly after the royal wedding, we had landed up at the Ship and with the help of a jug or two were putting the world to rights. Country Jack hadn't met Dan at that time but seemed to have heard of him and was anxious to make his aquaintance.

The Ship was a relatively safe place to discuss our past and future plans, which was just as well, for the drink soon opened our lips, and not too quietly either. But if you are not safe in a bawdy house in the criminal heart of London, where are you?

We need work that offers the maximum profit for the minimum danger," said Dan as if it was a litany learned by heart. I couldn't disagree with that.

"Now I am rested, I may return to the country," said Country Jack. "And I would be glad of a reliable partner who can ride well and handle a weapon. I am not saying I favour violence, mind. I would prefer to steal with a kiss than with a sword thrust. Which is more than can be said for many so-called gentlemen of the road."

At that he regaled us with a story that was current of a robbery on Hounslow Heath where four people had been most violently attacked. The two servants had been tied with bridle-straps to horses with their hands bound and their feet knotted to one another under the horses' bodies.

"Now that is what I call unnecessary," said Jack. "Those servants were as poor as the damned robbers and it would not be my way to treat them to such danger and discourtesy." He paused.

"Mind you, if they'd done that to the rich buggers..."
We all laughed and heartily agreed.

Then Dan spoke. "I would partner you, if you would take me with you."

That night, Dan came back to our lodgings and I tried to persuade him against this plan.

"You know this is a path to the gallows. They all end up there sooner or later. Even the butcher, Turpin will dangle in the end."

It seemed unlikely. Turpin and Rowden moved openly around the country. They even came to London from time to time, but there was no-one prepared to arrest them though everyone knew they were there.

"Before I return and claim Mudge, I must have the wealth to do so." More pipe-dreams. I had helped him send a letter a week to this lady, and little had come back by way of any real encouragement.

"Then lower your sights - come in with us. Steal what is easy to steal and easy to pass on. Clothes, fabrics - there is such a demand at this time people will buy all we can purloin, no questions asked." But his mind was set and no amount of persuasion on my part would change it.

Country Jack, for his part, was determined to move apace and soon saw Dan kitted out for his new role. As he said, it was disrespectful to one's victims to dress like a ragamuffin, so there was a measure of lace and velvet to be paid for. Also two horses were acquired. I didn't like to ask how. But as they were embarking on a partnership that carried the death penalty if discovered, a couple of stolen horses in their possession was not likely to make a whole load of difference.

We saw them leave, my wife and I, Ann Evans, Elizabeth Shelton, the blacksmith Clarence Germane and a few other friends. And I genuinely believed that was the last I would see of him.

Chapter 14
The words of Country Jack ~ May 1734

The air was as still as a dead man's lips the morning we rode out of London. We were up early, but the street traders were earlier. Their cries echoed across East London.

"Here's pennyroyal and marigolds. Who will buy my water-cress?"
"Knives, scissors and razors to grind; old chairs to mend."
"My bell I keep ringing, and merrily singing, now buy my muffins."
"'ere's yer toys for girls an' boys"
"ol' clo'(thes)"

Hundreds of voices carried on the air competing for attention with the few already awake and about. There were those who said such sounds were to Londoners what the songs of larks and nightingales were to the likes of myself. But I could never see it. London was a place to hide when it was unsafe to be elsewhere, no more. And I knew my young colleague felt the same way.

I had not worked with a partner before, but recent experience had taught me another pair of eyes and a finger on the trigger would help make my life safer. It is true, I would have preferred a man with a little more presence about him. Dan Malden looked little more than a child, but at least he could ride - I'll say that for him. I have yet to encounter such a fine horseman.

He had told me he'd been a jockey and at one point when we ventured south into Kent, I caught him wistfully watching boys exercising racing horses on the downs above Canterbury.

"I'll do it again, you know," he said. "I'll have grand gen'lemen shake my hand and toast my success in fine claret." And I am sure he meant it.

Another time, he said, "Do you think this will make them remember me?" I didn't know what he was about. I preferred to remain as anonymous as those lost to the plague-pits, but he went on about it any number of times.

"I don't know what it will be, but something will make them remember me, long after we are all gone." As for myself, I was just content to see the next day dawn and find a profit in an encounter.

As a result, we took what we could wherever we could find it. Enough highwaymen had been arrested or killed along the roads around London to open up opportunities for those like ourselves. But we did not stay long enough in one place to acquire a reputation.

That month, we collected coin from those who had stopped to rest their horses at Clapham. On another occasion, we rode north to Epping and robbed a coach party of jewellery and silken handkerchiefs. We had silver plate and cutlery from a carriage we held at gunpoint near Turnham Green. And we even had the best of valuables being held aboard a boat at Chiswick.

Passing the proceeds of our endeavours was no problem. Pawnbrokers were not always too particular about questioning the source of a variety of items, provided the price was right. We took care not to return to the same place too often. The very best pieces, we kept in a safe place to take back to London on our return. We knew Annie Evans or Beth Shelton would find us the most grateful of buyers when the time was right. I remember the occasion when I first showed Dan where we were to store the booty. I think it caused us both some amusement.

It was after a small piece of opportunism on our part. We had been out to Romford. There had been a market and fair, and as was common, farmers had brought livestock for sale. Before their return home, most would celebrate their success with a drink or three in one of a number of hostelries. You could spot them a mile off - those with money to spend. The more they drank, the more careless they would become. It was almost too easy.

Holding up a coach at gunpoint is a violent act. It can be dangerous and you never quite know how your partner will react if things go wrong. To that point, I had never required Dan to shoot the pistol he had primed and aimed at our victims. Truly speaking, I had my doubts whether he was capable of shooting anybody.

An ass of a farmer with money almost falling out of his pockets was a far easier mark. After three pints of ale, into which I had surreptitiously dropped a measure of gin or two, he wasn't even remembering to button his pockets up. And when he made the inevitable visit outside, he even took off his jacket and hung it on the fence whilst he relieved himself into the stinking ditch below. Dan had the horses ready to make our escape, and half an hour later under cover of woodland and oncoming darkness, we examined our evening's work. The jacket itself was of no inherent value. It might fetch a few shillings with a Jewish trader. But the pockets yielded guineas and sovereigns, a fine watch, even some spectacles and a pocket pistol.

"We'll rest the night in the open and make for my store in the morning," I promised Dan.

"Your store?"

"We need a safe place to keep such things as we shall later return to London with. Get some sleep and I'll show you."

The temperature dropped that night and I didn't sleep well. I have spent many a night in the open, but since the unfortunate events of the previous year, the sword wound I had received would ache and throb if it became particularly cold. That was such a night and I was only too pleased to start early. Besides, I knew I had a surprise for my young accomplice..

There is a small village not ten miles from Chelmsford - I'll be no more specific than that - and it has a ruined church. Once, the parish thrived, but times changed and this church became - shall we say - unnecessary. Ivy claws its way across the brick and stone, covering whole windows. Parts of the roof are open to the sky. Where tiles remain, colonies of house-leeks thrive. There are those who say they prevent lightning striking a building and that is why people encourage their growth.

Within the church's silent walls, behind its chained and bolted doors lie all those ornaments you would associate with such a building. Oh, the silver plate and the tasselled altar cloths are gone, but other more permanent items remain. Stained glass panels, one or two, survive. The font and the pulpit are still there, though the wood of the latter has suffered greatly. And the chest is there - the great ornately carved parish chest is still there in a corner of the vestry. Like so many of its kind, it has three locks once governed by three keys - formerly in the charge of the parson and the two churchwardens.

What may not be clear to the eye is that two of those locks are now permanently jammed open, whilst the third is still governed by a single key, the key that hangs always around my neck.

It was still early morning and few were about when we rode through the village. The sun had risen early and it would be a fine and a pleasant day. It was a countryman's day; a long day for the ploughman; a day humming with the activity of birds and insects. Never was I more glad to be away from the city.

"This'll be a day to view the world from horseback," Dan commented. I knew exactly what he meant.

"Well, just a short ride first, then we can take ourselves where we will."

The church lay conveniently just away from the cluster of tenements that still tried to call itself a village. I knew one side door could be forced to open wide enough to afford entry to those thin as ourselves. This was the moment at which I felt a warning was necessary.

"I have never shown this secret to anyone." I paused. "I am not a vindictive man, but should you ever take advantage of the trust I am placing in you, then..."

I knew no more was necessary. We were, after all, men of honour.

"There is one other thing," I added. "Others known to you have been my life-savers." He nodded thinking I meant simply our colleagues in London. "Should you ever need to find me, I commonly return to this place and though this hiding place is known only to we two, others near here may let you know of my whereabouts."

"And would I ask for Country Jack?"

"Simply, Jack. It is safer that way and if you find the right person they will know to match the two of us."

I was not to know that there would come a time when such a subterfuge would prove valuable. In the meantime, we left it at that.

Within the chest, a few treasures remained from earlier visits. We deposited one or two more from our latest escapade, then, covering even our footprints, we left. Somehow I knew I could trust Dan Malden. There was comfort in a secret shared.

Around the middle of June that year we encountered Richard Turpin. I had no desire to trespass on another man's territory. But briefly, I wondered if I had done just that, and that I had violated the domain of none other than the butcher himself.

It was difficult to know where Turpin and the rest of the Essex gang were. If you believed the tales circulated in the newspapers, they were active on every road from Dover to Durham. If the truth be known, they could not have been responsible for half the robberies that bore their name. Too many thugs made use of the fear generated by the name, and sought to pass themselves off as Turpin. Nothing emptied pockets faster than threats from a man you believed to be Dick Turpin.

We were camped on the edge of Epping Forest when three of them rode up. They carried grim looks, though they were quite finely dressed and well mounted. Though I had never spoken to any of them face to face, I knew who they were. The man Turpin - the one they called 'The Butcher' could have been a gypsy, so dark was his complexion. He had flared, pox-marked cheeks and an upright stance. The other two I took to be brothers, probably two of the Gregory boys. What surprised me was Dan seemed to know them. Then, two others arrived, one of them a girl. She seemed really pleased to recognise Dan, and from then on I felt more at my ease.

"Well, cousin, here's a fine thing - I've read about highway robbers almost as famous as our little crew. None other than Country Jack and The Jockey."

This was the first I knew of our new notoriety. And though Dan had abandoned his jockey's cap in favour of more a distinguished outfit, his size and horsemanship had earned him a new nickname.

"Our days of such trade may be short," said Turpin. He didn't speak much, but seemed anxious we should know this.

"I think I may take up military service awhile and take to the sea."

"I have tried that ," said Dan, "and prefer it as I am now."

"Should any ask," insisted Turpin, "the butcher has enlisted and gone to the Low Country."

They stayed but a short time, and then were gone. It was the last I ever saw any of them alive.

Soon after that, Dan and I suffered a fright. We were shot at from inside a coach that we had stopped, and left in a hurry penniless. We then decided to recover our cache of valuables and realise their worth. Dan was anxious to return to Ipswich. He told me there was a woman he hankered after, and it was clear there was to be no shaking him over this. So we were minded to share our wealth and then to part. We had been together just eight weeks.

Carrying the items we had brought from the old church, we felt more vulnerable than usual, so entering Whitechapel, we carried on down to Gracechurch Street, just short of London Bridge. It was there we put up at an inn under the sign of the Cross Keys. It would not have been my choice. It was a busy coaching inn and you always have coaches leaving at inconvenient hours with all the noise that entails. It was not the place you would choose for a good night's sleep. We had been on the road for several hours and could afford more comfort than that, but the place had its advantages. It was close to one of the properties owned by Elizabeth Shelton. It was arranged she should meet us on our arrival and inspect what we had to sell.

With so many people coming and going, we were unlikely to be noticed or recognised. On arrival, we made sure we were fed and we waited. When Beth Shelton arrived, she was impressed with what we had to offer and was convinced much of it could be placed in but a short time. Prices were spoken of and certain items taken away. As for ourselves, we were tired and took to our beds early. Even the sounds of coaches departing at three o'clock in the morning were not enough to interrupt our exhaustion.

The next thing I recall was waking to a screaming and a smell of smoke. Horses were kicking against panels in their stalls and I distinctly caught the word, "fire!"

I looked to the other bed. Dan was already awake and moving. I grabbed for the bags containing such valuables as were still in my possession and made towards the door. Smoke filled the first stairway and we found it easier to head towards the front staircase.

As it later became evident, a servant had left a candle burning close to some bedding. This had ignited and within minutes, the place was an inferno. Most of the guests had already left on coaches, but there was much to be done. In the yard, horses were stabled, though fire and smoke made an impenetrable wall in one section. The cries of the animals trapped were terrible to hear. But we were distracted by other cries.

There was a barber's shop in the yard and the apprentices had been locked in by their master. Grabbing an axe from a woodpile, Dan hacked at the door. As it came free from its lock, I must have counted three young lads, running to safety. People were rushing in all directions, calling, yelling, crying.

A group of women were encouraging an elderly man, trapped two floors up, to jump, which he eventually did, they endeavouring to break his fall. That fortunate man walked away with no harm done to him, save the fright. It was the fright that put a woman in a nearby house into a labour several weeks before her time, and they do say she miscarried the same day and her life was put in great danger.

It seemed as if all were out that could be rescued, but much more was to be done. If the whole of that part of London was not to be aflame we had to quench the fire, and water was brought in any carrier large enough to make a difference. Many ran to the river's edge to bring water. It was a few hundred yards away, but as carts and barrows arrived from all areas around, we could begin to contain the fire. Backing onto the yard were about a dozen dwellings. Their tenants were desperately working against the flame to save their homes. Dan and I meanwhile were focused on the warehouses that formed another side of the square beside the inn. We knew Elizabeth Shelton's was one of those. All that could be done to save life had been done. Now the property of a friend assumed a special importance. A small wagon stood in the yard that had been used for transporting coals from the docks.

"Come on," called Dan. "We can use this for fetching water." I couldn't see how. It was made from roughly hewn planks.

"But the water will just run through."

"Use your imagination!" he yelled.

And still unable to see what use it could possibly be, I found myself pushing the cart with him down Gracechurch Street and Fish Street to the Bridge. There was a slipway to the water beside the bridge, where in spite of others trying to access the river, we pushed our way past, right into the river itself. The tide was low and a thick clay-like mud was exposed.

Dan called to me, "Come on, like this!"

And he began plastering up the cracks between the boards with the clay. We slopped the clay around all corners of the cart and others who may or may not have understood our purpose helped us. When it seemed watertight, we ran the cart right into the river to fill it. It then needed the combined efforts of a number of us to bring the cart back to street level and pull and push it back to the Cross Keys.

"Over here," called a warehouse owner, anxious to preserve his property. But we ignored his pleas and went to the end where Beth Shelton's store was and began bucketing water onto anywhere that needed it. We went on like that all morning until the fire was out. It took several hundred of us at least six hours, and the final bill ran to many thousands of pounds, but I am proud to say, we saved that storehouse.

There were lives lost. One lady, who was known for wearing an iron girdle on account of her disability, was later discovered. All that remained to identify her was the iron girdle. A gentleman who lodged there was also missing. But I like to believe he made his escape and used the fire to disguise his continued existence elsewhere. I can see the advantage of being able to arrange such a disappearance.

Much property burned. The inn was completely destroyed along with the warehouses of goods belonging to a number of traders. A wagon loaded with goods just about to depart was lost, as were six horses belonging to the Sudbury carrier.

When she heard of Dan's part in saving her premises, Elizabeth Shelton was full of praise and gratitude. More than that, she said she was indebted to Dan, for surely without his help her goods would have been destroyed. And much of what she had, she could never have admitted to owning. It would become of some significance later what Beth Shelton said to my young colleague that morning.

"If ever you need my help at any time, you only need to ask. London is a harsh place to need to seek help. You can depend on mine whenever or for whatever reason you come calling."

Chapter 15
The words of Mary Malden, otherwise known as Mudge ~ Summer 1734 and on into 1735

How I came to find myself in that dreadful place, I shall never know. But I suppose I wanted a marriage and that was likely to be the best on offer. Not even a proper chapel, but a damp and foul-smelling cellar with a drunken slob of a parson, if parson he ever was. Like so many others at that time, I was to be a Fleet bride. No pageantry, little Christianity, but a simple ceremony at the sign of the 'Hand and Pen' in the shadow of the debtors' prison.

Dan had turned up quite out of the blue, seemingly wealthy. Though I had moved twice since I had last seen him and most of his letters had failed to find me, he knew where to look - close enough to the quay to smell the fish as it came ashore and never too far from the last set of sailors to disembark.

He seemed to have grown in confidence. And this time he was promising to make an honest woman of me. So I fell for it. I wasn't getting any younger, you see, and I always had a soft spot for Dan Malden. Leaving most matters in Ipswich unresolved and with barely an acknowlegement to his parents he had been there, I was off to London for the second time. I never did tell him about my first visit, though he did tell me he had lived with this woman who had died even though he had never truly stopped loving me.

When we entered the place where he'd been living, it was as if I lost all control of my life. Imagine yourself in a bar surrounded by people you don't know, talking about places and events outside your experience. That is precisely how I found myself, just hours after arriving.

"You want to save your money - a Fleet wedding can be had for half a crown." That was Clarence Germane, the blacksmith.

"But is it a real wedding?" I wanted to ask.

As if sensing my concern, a lady I came to know as Ann Evans assured me, that it would be conducted by the learned Doctor T.C. and our names would be entered into the 'true and ancient register.' There was much nodding of heads and before I knew it I was off in my best attire to what can best be described as a hole in the ground where a drunken cleric struggled to remember his lines. As we emerged into the light, I became aware of the existence of a number of these establishments that had grown up around the old prison, many of which were attached to public houses. There were touts approaching anyone of marriageable age trying to lure custom into their favoured hostelry. When they learned we were already just married, their comments assumed a more ribald nature.

To this day I am still unsure as to whether we were ever truly married. All I know is from then on I regarded myself, and was addressed by others, as Mrs. Malden, or Morgan, or Moulding or Smith or whatever alias that rascal was operating under at the time.

One thing I will say for Dan, life with him was never dull. I understood that much of the money he had come by was as a result of unlawful activity. I knew that sooner or later, I would be tarred with the same brush but, to be honest, I was ever the eager partner and never the reluctant bride. You see, those times were amongst the happiest of my life, and though we could flip from calm and a contentment one minute to hurling insults at one another the next, I knew he cared for me as I did for him. Added to which it was fun.

We sat one night in the Ship with John Holburt and his wife. I liked her. There was no side to her. But he always seemed to want to appear grander than he truly was. I know nothing of his origins, but he had been educated and liked you to know it. He used words and phrases such as someone grander might have done though I doubt he was ever closer to a Dukedom than any of us.

There was a noisy party in the next stall. I could hear one voice well above the rest.

"I'll beg you to attend to your own business. I pride myself on being the best-dressed man in this part of London!"

At first, we weren't sure what this was all about, but whatever had been our own conversation dried up as we listened to this man, well-oiled by drink, ranting about the price he had paid for his periwig, his silk stockings and even the buckles on his shoes.

"Fashions come and fashions will go, but a man clothed simply but well will always be in the height of fashion."

Holburt's wife Ann began to titter. She popped her head over the stall to catch a glimpse of the man. Then, darting back almost unable to contain herself, she collapsed in laughter. One by one, we each took a look, then joined her. That one so seemingly ridiculous should be so puffed up with self-importance put us all in good humour.

"I have had titled gentlemen ask me for the name of my tailor. And I'll have you know, I only apply the finest powder as recommended by peruke-maker to His Majesty."

There were guffaws from the other side of the wooden partition. Even his own friends found it hard to take this man seriously.

"You know who that is?" Holburt said to Dan and myself. "That is old MacNeal: he has a yard servicing ships along the river. He lives just the other side of Salt-Petre Bank in East Smithfield. Why don't we teach him a lesson and benefit ourselves at one and the same time."

We sat listening further to the man's ranting and boasting till, bored and irritated, his friends drifted off. Slightly staggering, MacNeal straightened his periwig, put on his hat and launched himself in the direction of his home. We followed until, comfortably away from the square and no longer overlooked by houses, this puffed-up little man stooped to draw breath. Then all of a sudden, John had him on the floor and was whispering all manner of threats in the man's ear.

"You try to catch a look at us and it'll be the worse for you, you understand?"

Maybe it was the drink or the excitement of the moment, but I found myself whispering in that pathetic little man's ear, "Oh and us ladies can be far worse than the men when it comes to taking our revenge." And I grabbed him - where it hurts - well, it certainly hurt the way I grabbed him, but though he cried out, he didn't dare to unfasten his eyes, which stayed firmly and tightly shut.

After that he lay there quaking as we stripped him - yes, we stripped him bare as ever he was born, and scuttled away into the darkness with his wig and his hat, his coat, shirt and his silk stockings. I carried his shoes, complete with tasteless base-metal buckles. We even had his last five shillings, all that was left after his drinking session.

I heard later that he had knocked on the door of the first house he could find with a light still burning and they had taken him in. He couldn't say who had robbed him and even after Dan had much later made a full confession of all his crimes, it proved impossible to find anyone guilty of the offence. I couldn't feel sorry for the man. If this was what it meant to embark on a life of crime, then I was all for it. We made a few pounds for ourselves that night and had taken a rise out of the most contemptuous character possible.

When it came time to realise a profit on the affair, it was down the lane we headed - not straight away - but leaving a sensible and a safe time between the theft and the sale of the proceeds. It was easy and it bonded us together as group. There was a trust and a friendship there, whatever the shortcomings of some of the individuals involved,

That summer, we moved to Kent. It seemed half London was going with us. There was work in the hayfields, the harvests and the fruit farms. Work, that is, for me. Dan disappeared to Canterbury and Ashford where the races were run. He was enticed by the horses and the racing, convinced he still had a future as a jockey. For weeks, I worked long hours in the fields, putting by what I could.

He reappeared one evening in August. He was wearing that old jockey cap again. I had not seen it in years. He looked well-fed - broader, more affluent.

"What did I tell yer! I haven't lost the touch."

And then he proceeded to tell me how, after several weeks of stable-ladding, he had had his chance to ride, and come away successful. After that, two further wins had reinforced his reputation.

"If I come back next season, they'll give me more rides - not just races, but gen'lemen's challenges most likely. You'll see - they'll remember me."

We did not stay for the apple season. There was no need. We had enough to see us through the winter whilst Dan 'reviewed his options' as he described it. We came back to London. We were not the only ones. One day, bold as brass, in walked Country Jack. He was as surprised to see me as I was him. And Dan was more surprised than the pair of us to realise we had met before. Country Jack had the sensitivity to keep it to himself that we had also encountered one another in London. He merely told of how Harry and I had cared for him when his life hung in the balance. It was taken as the coincidence it was, a chance encounter that had served to bring us closer together.

"I must lay low awhile," Jack said. "There is a conspiracy among the magistrates, the constables and even the watch to bring those like myself before the courts. The time of leaving your crime and your criminal reputation behind you is slipping away. Before long, even those seemingly beyond the law may find they are entrapped by it."

Those words were truly prophetic, as before the end of the following year, many of those most deeply feared by travellers far and wide were presented before the courts and condemned.

It was a winter to stay indoors and hope you were as safe as houses. Unfortunately for many of our neighbours that was not safe enough, as in January we suffered the worst tempest of my lifetime. Many of our friends had to seek shelter with us whilst their homes were made habitable. I was surprised to learn that the same sense of community existed in our little enclave that I had known in Ipswich and even in the parish of my birth.

Before the spring had announced itself, the trials began. The seemingly untouchable Essex gang were routed. The Gregory brothers were all taken, two hanged and one shot. Joseph Rose and a number of his colleagues in crime were tried, executed and gibbeted at Edgeware. It seemed there was no hiding place for those who had dedicated their lives to crime. Even old Humphrey Walker, the oldest member of the gang, was beaten so badly in prison that he died of his wounds. He may have cheated the hangman, but it didn't stop them hanging his body up for the crowds to gawp at and the crows to pick clean.

Around that time we heard that Mary Brazier had been indicted and sentenced to death. But she did not hang. Her appeal for mercy had not gone unheeded and in anticipation of her transportation to the American colonies, we went to see her in prison. She was a pale shadow of the brash and brazen hussy of before. I almost felt sorry for her.

"Stay clear of all this," she begged Dan. "Or you'll get the same as Joe. It makes no difference whether you steal a rich man's gold watch or a poor man's stockings, they'll hang you or banish you to a life of hard labour. Take my advice. Leave it and be an honest man whatever the cost may be in terms of poverty and destitution."

Though it would be some time before the punishment ship carried her off, we could not bring ourselves to visit her again. It was all too upsetting.

It wasn't only the Essex gang that met their come-uppance. The notorious Thomas Winter was taken later that year and was tortured to such an extent that he impeached twenty of his gang as well as confessing to a murder and thirty-six robberies. The man William Blackwell, known as Long Will, also was arrested and hanged in chains.

Winter behind us, it was time to leave the city. Dan was convinced that another summer in Kent would see him making his fortune as a jockey. He was so sure people would remember him, but he was to be bitterly disappointed. There were few rides to be had. It wasn't all bad news. I found work in the fields and he came back to find me one day dressed in an outfit the like of which I'd never seen.

"And where do you think you stole that fancy rig?"

"It's not stolen - it's my new work attire," he grinned.

There was more gold braid than on a cathedral altar-cloth.

"And what sort of work sets you out like that?"

"I'm a postillion."

"No? But you need to know about things like that..."

"I do; well, at least I'm good with horses and I know where I want 'em to go, so it can't be that difficult to make 'em do what I want 'em to do. You see I said they'd remember me, and they did."

"Do they know you 'in't never been a coachman before?"

"What they don't know don't matter, jus' so long as I can do the work."

And for a few weeks it went well, though I know he'd have sooner been riding in races. He rode one of the lead horses in a team of four, sometimes with a coachman driving them, sometimes with another postillion astride one of the 'wheelers' behind.

Unfortunately, it was not always like that. Too much of his time was spent back at the coaching inn, with his braided uniform hung away, cleaning out the stables like any common stable lad.

We knew we would be returning to hard times in London, and with the remains of summer's miserly earnings, we came back to discover all was not well in our little community.

There had been more arrests, with the likelihood of more to follow. Country Jack had the sense to vanish. Yet Turpin and Rowden contemptuously rode openly in places where they were known and continued to pose a threat to travellers of means. For all that, even their time at liberty was under threat. Parishes around the capital had strengthened the watch and armed guards travelled on many coaches. Groups from the military and the Militia rooted out smugglers, highwaymen and the like. Cornet and drum sounded through the squares of London as Lord Mark Kerr's Regiment of Dragoons imposed a kind of martial law on the land. If thieves slept comfortably in their beds it was because it was about the only place they were likely to remain safe.

They do say, a year and a day will make a Londoner of you. I had been there all of that and more, and it hadn't become any easier. That winter just made things worse. As our funds dwindled, we traded in clothes and fabrics. Dan, along with John Holburt and his wife would raid the drying lines of big houses or the laundries of the ladies who washed for them. If there were identifing marks on the fabrics, they were cut off and stitched up. There was always a strong demand for fine fabrics. Sheets would arrive, often still damp. I would dry them and search them for monograms, making any adjustments necessary. Before long, it seemed our output was greater than a good-sized mill. But, of course, even our little enterprise could hardly go unnoticed forever.

Chapter 16
The words of John Holburt ~ Winter 1735

I remember that winter as being very harsh. It began with a biting chill to the wind and concluded with high tides and a great inundation. Added to that, a distemper came to our part of London that was such that at times there were barely enough in fair health to nurse the sick. It meant, of course, there were fewer to guard the streets and as I recall, all manner of audacious crimes were enacted.

One man dressed in the livery of a ticket-porter delivered a letter to a wealthy surgeon with orders to come and bleed one of his patients who lived in Bloomsbury. On dismounting from his carriage, he was set upon by three footpads who relieved him of his watch, two guineas and case of medical instruments.

Grave robbers were at work in Stepney and Islington. Grave-diggers would tip off the medical men when good clean bodies might be had at dead of night, and by morning, newly interred bodies had been spirited away, as if resurrected.

One crime that gave us all a chuckle was when a number of the pewter signs from the inns around Whitechapel disappeared within one week. The watch was doubled, but by then it was too late of course. The landlady of the Seven Stairs in Petticoat Lane was furious. She had only just installed a new one. And then they came on offer to Beth Shelton. She took them. When the parish constables came with a warrant, as they did from time to time, all they found was the metal. One lump of melted pewter looks much the same as another. She even had a stamp that she'd used to make it look legal.

There may have been attempts to clamp down on crime, but it still went on. There were lanes and corners in our part of the world where no watchman would dare to set foot; dark alleys that came to be known by such descriptions as 'Cut-throat Court' and

'Gulley's end.'

It was as much as a form of protection as anything else, that our little band stuck together. Protection from the authorities that might discover too much about our activities, and protection against the street gangs of our time who cared little who they might hurt. There were a lot of Irish in our neighbourhood and though most were decent enough, a few were best avoided, especially when the drink was in them, which was most of the time. The Irish were prepared to take on unpleasant and dangerous work, for wages that true Londoners would have turned up their noses at. So there was an uneasy distance between the two communities, many of the unemployed believing it was the Paddies who were taking their jobs.

We never regarded ourselves as a gang; just a tight-knit group of friends that sometimes chose to work together, other times apart. Some, like Country Jack drifted in and out of the neighbourhood as fancy took them, but that was alright with us. We knew we could rely on one another and only under extreme provocation would we have betrayed one another.

I know now that when Dan Malden implicated me, it was as a result of what they did to him. I am sure I would have behaved in the same way under such threats. But I'm getting ahead of myself. As we came to the end of 1735, our little band was never so united. We would meet for long drinking sessions in one of a number of hostelries, 'mending material matters' and planning our schemes.

That winter, there were the wagers... challenges which could be foolhardy, often dangerous. Who could steal something, then sell the same item back to its owner? I had to do that one. And I was successful. A fool of a wine-cooper who had no idea of what he had laid down couldn't even recognise what he had bought (probably from a smuggler) some years earlier and was only too pleased to buy a gallon of his own best Canary from me for four shillings.

The best challenge involved that woman of Dan Malden's

- Mudge they called her. I liked her - she had spirit. As usual, it was after a long drinking session this 'dare' came about.

"I reckon, as all the highwaymen have been taken, it'll be up to the women to take their turn," laughed Dan.

He was joking, of course.

"I suppose you think we women couldn't manage it?" she replied.

"Well, I've not heard of that many highway*women*," Dan quipped.

After that, she was bound to take up the challenge. She had that sort of vigour about her and though she must have known the nature of what she was about to undertake, she was determined to prove to us all that she could do it.

Now, stealing a little laundry and concealing it under your dress is one thing, but robbing a man in daylight on the open road is another. So many go armed these days, with pistols or leaden sticks. When Dan realised she was serious, he was intent on helping her, but she was having none of it - she could do it as well as any man, she said, including the mighty Turpin.

So it was the two of them took themselves well away beyond Romford and out towards Ingatestone. What I know of the affair comes to me as much from the intelligence published in *Bagnall's News* as from their description on their return.

They had hired horses, good ones at that, in case of the need to make a fast getaway. They were well-dressed and had disguised their features with the aid of black crapes. They each had a gun, though I doubt Mudge had ever fired one in anger before.

Separating as they spotted a lone traveller, it was left to Mudge to challenge the man. He was a local wholesale butcher. The fellow was quite taken aback at the sight of an elegant woman seated side-saddle pointing a pistol at him and demanding he hand over his money.

"Madam," he replied, "I am amazed at such behaviour in one of your sex and do not understand what you mean."

Dan, sensing things were not going to plan, approached and chastised the man.

"Sir, you are a brute to make any hesitation in granting what a lady requests of you. " And he swore D____n his B____d, if he did not immediately gratify her desire, he would shoot him through the head.

The butcher then realised they were both serious, thought better of further protest and handed over his watch, six guineas and some silver.

"The man was most compliant," laughed Mudge as she displayed her gains to us all the following day. She was well applauded by our little team. Oh yes, there was a camaraderie there that transcended all the hardships we were later to endure.

In the month of November, it was the anniversary of the King's birthday. Suffice it to say, we were not invited to the celebrations. But as I recall, a number of us found ourselves caught up in the crowds that had gathered around St. James to view those so honoured, arriving to take part in the festivities. It had not been our intention to pay court to a set of aristocratic peacocks such as were on show that day, but finding ourselves close to some of the coaches arriving, we stopped to marvel. And you had to admit, it was a remarkable scene. So many carriages had arrived at once, there was little chance for many of them to set down their occupants anywhere near the Royal Court, so they were forced to alight at a distance affording the assembled multitudes a fine view of their costume.

Many of the gentlemen wore brown-coloured flowered velvets, or dark cloth coats laced with gold or silver. Their westcoats were either of gold stuffs or of rich flowered silks of a large pattern on a white ground. Many had open sleeves to their coats. Their wigs were with large curls setting forward and rising from the forehead and the tyes they sported were thick and black and prominent. I notice these things, you see, since I began dealing in richer quality materials.

That was the real reason we were there, the four of us: Dan Malden and his woman, my wife Anne and myself. Beth Shelton had a quantity of finer fabrics to sell. And it was not stolen - well, not really. I believe it to have been the result of a wreck off the Kent coast that had somehow found its way to her. Such a gathering of people of all classes was too good an opportunity to miss. It had been our intention to spread ourselves among the crowd, offering what we had to anyone keen to dress themselves more finely than they could commonly afford.

But it was somehow compelling just to look upon those arriving to His Majesty's court. And whilst the gentlemen may have been figures of fascination, it was the ladies who really drew one's attention. Their gowns were of the finest silks with wide short sleeves, short petticoats and their stays very low before. Some had gold and silver nets on their petticoats and gold and silver set into their sleeves like flounces. They wore fine scalloped laced heads, many with hair curled down on the sides, tied with cockades of riband or silken flowers. Diamond rings and necklaces were worn and even the men sported diamond buckles in their shoes, giving the appearance of great fortunes... which of course is exactly what they were intended to do.

We did well that day, for though our attention had been drawn away from the task we had been set, the fact we felt envy at such a conspicuous display of wealth, meant that others must feel that way too. What we had to trade may have been several shades in value and taste beneath what had stepped from those carriages, but it was exactly what many of our customers were bound to be drawn to. It was as near to grandeur as they were ever likely to aspire again. So our fabrics sold like hot muffins on an autumn evening.

Which is why our little band liked to set our sights on becoming honest traders of such stuff. Late into the November night, we planned how we might begin, through less legitimate activities, eventually to supply a demand that would come from all classes and levels of society.

"Would that we had permanent supply of grand fabrics and adornments," Dan Malden said.

"But not so grand that we discourage the crowds that were our customers tonight," I added.

"I fear," replied Dan Malden's wife, "that any legitimate trade practised by this crew of ours would soon make us as mean and wretched as the poorest Jew at Rag Fair. Our way is not destined to be like that, and I think we have to take things as they are rather than how they might once have been."

It was the most serious speech made that night and in the light of everything that followed, probably the most meaningful. But for the time being, such philosophy was lost in the raucous exchange of the beer house.

Chapter 17
The words of Dan Malden ~ February 1736

There are parts of this story that only I can tell, and though I never learned to pen words with any real efficiency, rest assured these are my words and mine alone, as told to others in our little company. There were several of us... John Holburt and his wife, Ann, Mudge and myself. There was Country Jack when he was there, but he came and went with the frequency, though less regularity than the tide. There was Beth Shelton and Annie Evans who handled and sold on such goods as fell into our hands. And there were others on the fringes, like Germane the blacksmith, who had peculiar talents like the ability to melt or beat metal in such ways it could no longer be recognised.

There was also Thomas George - not too intelligent as I recall, so most of the time we left him out of our business. He was unreliable - like the evening in January when we were drinking in Joseph Silvester's house, the Magpye. For once, Country Jack was there. Otherwise, I was on my own; Mudge having gone to help Beth Shelton with a consignment of cloth from a questionable source, down Limehouse way. Unsure of its origins, the ladies had decided the safest way to handle it was to smoke it over brimstone to cleanse it. It was an unpleasant task, but a necessary one. I was glad to be out of it.

I am not quite sure how it came about, but we called for drink, without being sure who was paying. Tom George received his in a pot of some value. It was a quart pot - a heavy one and stamped to show it was solid silver.

"Do you reckon the ol' bugger knows what he's got here?" asked Tom.

"Like as not, he just thinks its a regular pewter pot," said Country Jack.

It seemed possible. Whether any of us had the money to

pay for our drinks is uncertain. Either way, it became irrelevant as we took it upon ourselves to down the contents of our mugs and a few more before walking out of that house, Tom still clutching the silver mug, finishing his drink as he went.

We had been 'dealing' with any amount of silver that winter - salts, tankards, spoons and plates, and regarded ourselves as experts on such matters. The next day, Tom and Ann Evans tried a few dealers to give them a price on the mug. But word was already out from Goldsmith's Hall, and when they finally sold it somewhere in the Minories for under five pounds, the constables started searching for us all.

Tom, living in Islington not far from the Magpye, was taken. Country Jack did what Country Jack was best at, and went into hiding. I had no need, as nobody was going looking in Whitechapel for an accomplice when they had the thief already in custody. But Ann Evans was already under observation, such was her notoriety. She was fined four shillings and tenpence for her part in the affair. They fined Thomas George thirty-nine shillings for simple grand larceny as it was his first offence. Had it not been, they'd have transported him. It could have worked out worse, but it was careless of all of us and it put our names before the judges. Which meant that when we were later indicted, we could hardly claim we were new to the profession.

As I said, much of our business involved fabrics of all kinds, and the more audacious our means of acquiring them the more I enjoyed it. Those were good times. I felt I belonged in a way that I had not at any time in my life since those days of my boyhood on the banks of the Orwell.

A little west and to the north of where we dwelt were the big houses of Islington and Holloway. Oh there were plenty there just as poor as ourselves, and worse, but behind high walls there was also great wealth. These were people who did not expect to wash and clean for themselves and they employed armies of servants to be subservient. Those who did not want their houses invaded by the lower classes sent out their laundry and only employed day staff.

A woman named Mary Henshaw had established a successful business washing for the well-heeled. She had once been comfortably off herself, living in a big house and married to a merchant in the city. But the debts that had come to light following his death had cast her into penury, and in an attempt to keep her big house and re-establish her way of life, she had put the space to good use. Rows of tubs covered the once polished floors and other people's sheets and shirts hung in her gardens drying. Of course a lady like her didn't do much of the scrubbing herself - she was far too busy entertaining her lady friends. So lines of young girls could be found six days a week (seven, if the work was there) washing, scrubbing and rinsing the linen of the near-gentry.

I came to know of this when drinking at the Castle at Holloway, a favourite tavern of mine at the time.

"Lucy! Well I never!" I spotted an old friend - well, not so much a friend as an employee - one of the girls I had managed about two years earlier. She looked pretty and vivacious as ever and I was somewhat surprised to learn that she was no longer 'on the game.'

"No, Mr. Daniel, I'm a proper laundress now," she proudly announced. "Though I could make an exception if you was interested."

"Were it not for the fact I am married..." I began.

"Married!" she shrieked. "Not to that Polly girl?"

"No, not to her - she died. No, I am married to an old friend from Ipswich. So, much as you are every part the temptation you ever were, I am afraid I shall have to decline your kind invitation."

Well, then she wanted to know all about what I was doing. I was cautious, naturally. But as she was far keener to tell me all about her new employment, that was not really a problem.

"There's quite a few of us 'courtesans.'

That was laugh. You could hardly have called any of our

girls courtesans. But it seemed that some of the better class whores had gone that way too. This Henshaw woman saw herself as a real do-gooder and had recruited her workers from some of the smarter street girls. Provided they stayed sober, clean, worked hard and were honest, she promised to help them make a new life for themselves.

"And we only handle the best linens and cotton fabrics. Some of our customers are titled ladies and gentlemen."

I doubted that, but my ears had pricked up as I could see this as a possible source of supply. Lucy continued to regale me with details of their various customers and their washing. Sunday was usually a day of rest, though much was delivered for washing on a Saturday. My mind was a whirr. This meant that a choice of fine sheets and clothing would be available to anyone making entry to that kitchen on a Sunday night.

"What sort of woman is this Mary Henshaw?" I asked. "Does she have men staying with her at the house? Or does she drink alone."

"Good Lord, neither is true! She is a most sober woman; but one not to be crossed," said Lucy. "I have seen her reduce the strongest of street girls to tears with little more than a glance. She takes pride in her continence and expects only the highest moral standards of others. On Sunday she attends church twice and is always early to bed to prepare herself for the rigours of the day ahead."

This was of more than casual interest to me and I left Lucy, promising to make her acquaintance again. Later that week, I went with Mudge to view the scene of what I saw as our next crime. I chose the middle of the week, as business would be slight. We took a shirt, a shift and an apron for washing. Mudge occupied her with conversation whilst I walked around inside observing the casements and how best one might effect an entry.

I thought my interest had gone unnoticed, but that woman has eyes like a hawk and I fear I had already aroused her worst suspicions.

Our merry crew heard of our visit to the Henshaw woman's house with interest. The day we had been, fine clothing and bedding was laid out drying across the kitchen. There would have been many pounds in value from a raid that day. But we had to bide our time a little. It was two days later, just before the end of February, when John Holburt and I, along with our wives, took up residence with Thomas George who only lived only a few streets from Mary Henshaw's house. He was friendly with one Mary Gray who had promised to handle the proceeds of this expedition. She offered the convenience of regularly dealing in household fabrics. She lived down along the Ratcliffe Highway.

On the Sunday, after Henshaw had returned from morning service, we went to collect our laundry. It gave me another chance to view the casements, this time from the outside as we walked away.

"How fine your garden looks," I found myself saying. But it was all a device to amble closer to the kitchen windows to observe the shutters and to observe how firmly they were fixed.

It was dark, the wrong side of midnight and few were about. Cats got under your feet and there were watchmen to be avoided, but it was not well-patrolled, being a cold and unpleasant winter's night. Also, by chance, there was a particularly high tide that weekend, combined with a great inundation. Flooding was feared along the shores of the river and large numbers had gone either to save or to salvage.

Entering the garden by a side gate, the four of us were soon gathered outside the kitchen window. We had a crowbar to force the shutters by wrenching the pins but had not accounted for them to be keyed on the inside. Fortunately, we had brought other tools just in case of difficulties. We cut a way through the shutter, opened the casement and entered the kitchen. This time, I must admit the haul proved a little disappointing. We took all we could find. Later, it was to be listed as seven pairs of sheets, a dozen or more aprons and one shirt. The washing was still wet. We arrived back cold and disappointed. The shirt, the best quality piece of all, had been dropped twice on the way back, so it carried dirt stains that would not have impressed the washer-woman.

Breaking into a house in the dead of night in this country is a capital offence. Had we known we were risking all our lives for seven pairs of sheets, we would surely have thought again.

As it was, it was done, and we returned to Mary Gray's lodging with no reason to believe there was anything to connect us with the housebreaking.

The following morning, we made light of it. Mary Gray said she would wash the shirt. She had us deliver the other items. We had no wish to be found in possession of them. Mudge took a liking to one of the aprons. What I did not know then was that she tucked it, still damp, under her clothes. Our deliveries took us in different directions, but there was a vague agreement to meet up at one of the taverns in the neighbourhood.

Later that morning, I was in the Fountain when a constable came in. I recognised him from his staff of office.

"Would you be Daniel Malden?" he asked. He had a piece of paper in his hand.

"No, constable. I am Dan Morgan," I answered. Then I saw her - Mary Henshaw, pointing at me, shouting at me, urging him to arrest me.

"That is the man, constable, whatever he might say his name is!" She was shouting louder than ever. "I would recognise that thieving whelp anywhere. Constable - do your duty."

"Daniel Malden, alias Daniel Morgan I have a warrant for your arrest on a charge of housebreaking." The constable stood between me and the door, and any thoughts I might have had of absconding vanished.

I then learned they had already taken Mudge at the Castle tavern at Holloway. I was later told Holburt and his wife were claiming I had been the one instrumental in organising the robbery. What I did not know then was that Holburt had escaped and was still at large, but a search was out for him. Our latest lodgings had been searched and also that of Mary Gray, where she was found, still washing the dirty shirt.

Neighbours too had been subject to the search warrant. Holburt's rooms had yielded some of the sheets, still drying. Worse still, Mudge had been searched and the apron she had so wanted to keep, found, still damp underneath her own garments.

By late afternoon, all five of us appeared before Justice Robe at the Sessions House of the Old Bailey, and charged: four of us with housebreaking; Mary Gray with receiving one shirt.

Witnesses were drawn from our colleagues and associates, and suddenly all the trust I believed existed, melted away. John Banford who had been keen to purchase the linen when it was dry spoke damningly of me. Holburt and his wife somehow found the language to divorce themselves from most of the accusations. I had little to bargain with, but under severe provocation I admitted my part in the crime. I did not understand much of what I was accused and in all likelihood implicated others in that and other crimes. It was not my intention, but I want you to know I was shocked at my treatment. Accounts of my court experiences, reported in the newspapers later, described me as having my front teeth missing. That may give some people a clue as to why I made some of the statements I did under oath. I told them about the highway robbery of Daniel MacNeal a year before. To be honest, I probably confessed to starting the Great Fire and running up the National Debt, such was the treatment I received at the hands of those men. I was required to plead, and by that it did not mean a plea of 'not guilty.' No, I was taken to the Press Yard and shown those instruments of torture. I knew in no uncertain terms that if I failed to give them the answers they wanted, I would be stripped of all my clothes save those to cover my privy member and laid on the cold ground, limbs tied as if in crucifixion; then as much iron and stone would be piled upon me until I could bear it no more. And if I still refused to confess and to plead, I would be fed nothing more than dry crusts and water and the punishment repeated until I yielded or died.

Justice Robe, for all his finery, was no better. When the apron was found on Mudge's person, she was threatened if she didn't plead guilty she would face having her thumbs drawn with whip-cord. All this in pursuit of justice!

So it was, the four of us were taken and held under the securest lock and key and chain in a dark and depressing corner of Newgate Gaol, pending our trial. It is a dreadful place to behold, four floors high, dark and forbidding. When you enter through that gateway it is like entering the path to the dungeon of the firmest securest castle. Some called it the Sly House on account of all those who entered its portals but never came out.

We were there nine weeks. Then, the day came when we were paraded before the court, witnesses called and statements read out. None of it seemed to show any of us in a favourable light. Holburt spoke at some length to the jury and I could see he was winning them over. I am afraid I had none of his gift of persuasion. I stood by as others diced with my life. And at the end when the verdicts were announced, they all walked free. All but for me. How that could be, I can't imagine. Mary Gray was found washing one of the shirts we had stolen. Mudge was wearing one of the aprons, still damp around her waist. Yet they walked free and I was left for sentencing.

I can tell you now, those five days before the judge recalled us were the most terrible of my life. I was told to expect the worst, and the worst was what I got. Though London courts were unfamiliar with my face, my name had been spoken of a number of times, so mercy was not on the agenda. Sixty-seven of us were recalled to be told of our punishment. Just two were fined and imprisoned; fifty-eight were cast for transportation. Seven, including myself, received sentence of death. As the words were uttered, I became aware for the first time that others who knew me were in the courtroom. There were gasps, and I heard sobbing. I knew it was Mudge, though I could not bring myself to look at her.

Chapter 18
The words of Isaac Austen (warder at Newgate)
~ May 1736

They came and they went, and some even came back again, but I'll tell you one thing, that Dan Malden was no different from the rest of them. Funny that - I mean, mothers used to frighten their children with the very name of him as though he were some kind of figure of terror. Daniel Malden, the man who could break through brick walls and disappear without a trace. He could do that alright, but otherwise, he was much the same as our usual class of guest - scared, pathetic, a bit of a lost soul. He did at least have a few friends. Someone would turn up most days with food for him or for that woman of his. Sometimes it was pretty girls; sometimes it was characters I recognised by way of my professional dealings, you might say. As it was, I thought they were just fattening him up for the slaughter. I thought they'd probably hang the lot of them and good riddance too. But somehow, that Holburt had the tongue on him to distance himself from the crime he was obviously so guilty of. It wasn't the only time he would squeeze an acquittal out of an appointment with the hangman.

From what I heard, Dan Malden tried to take the blame away from that woman of his. If he did, it was probably the first gentlemanly thing he'd done in his life. After she was released, she came and sat with him a lot of the time. I had to watch she didn't pass him anything that might help him break out, but to tell you the truth, I didn't think he had it in him. He didn't really look the part of your master criminal - the height of nine penn'orth of coppers and scrawny with it - like a kid that had never really grown up. But then that was his advantage; he was wiry, strong in a determined sort of way. There was more about him than you'd ever have realised. There had to be for him to do what he did.

We had problems in the gaol at that time. There had been a number of attempted escapes, and the memory was still strong of the notorious Jack Sheppard. So bit by bit, the cells were being strengthened. But there were weaknesses, I had to admit. We had five prisoners due to hang at Tyburn on Monday May 24th that year, but there was also your usual cluster of bad boys along with any number due to be cast for transportation, so we were at stretching point, you might say.

There had been seven death sentences given out at that session, but His Lordship saw fit to reprieve two, so, five to hang, it was. There are limits to how many you can cram into the condemned hold. You have to be humane about this. The way I see it, these men are going to die and though there were some ruffians among them on that occasion, it did not seem right to condemn them to spend their last hours in utter squalor. Added to which, the Ordinary expects to spend time with them to make their peace with God and confess to all their countless misdemeanours. He would be far from happy to have to work in unnecessarily foul conditions. So we save our condemned cell for the chosen few. On this occasion, it was an arsonist by the name of Francis Owen, a housebreaker called George Ward and a burglar named Christopher Freeman. Dan Malden and a horse-thief, Thomas Tarlton were accommodated elsewhere among the master felons on the first floor.

It all happened the night before the hanging. It was a Sunday, and the Ordinary had been to each of the men in turn. Dan Malden seemed reluctant to make his final confession, seemingly convinced that the Governor, Mr. Akerman was about to announce his reprieve. There was no shaking him in this and all retired to bed. The Ordinary was dissatisfied as the printers were requiring the confessions to put in their broadsheets for sale to the crowds the next morning. He told them they would have to go and make it up which was what they usually did anyway.

The following morning, there was mayhem. When the guard arrived to escort the five prisoners to their final drop, one could not be found. Dan Malden had made his first escape from Newgate prison.

The route he had taken was, if not entirely original, an ingenious one. First, he had made loose the staple that held his irons. Then, observing that a plank was loose in the floor, had used the leg of a stool in his cell to prise up the plank, making a large enough arch under the floor for his body to slip through. In this way, he dropped into the cell below which was on the ground floor. As luck would have it, that cell was unoccupied, as a prisoner had escaped from it only days before by sawing through the window-bar. It had not been repaired. Being small, in spite of being encumbered by his irons, he slipped out of the window and into the part of the Press Yard where the prisoners could be exercised. There is a staircase from that yard up to the Chapel on the third floor. I surmise that he had already observed a breach in the Chapel wall. He waited till all was still in the yard. Then, removing his shoes, he climbed the staircase. I think he took them off in order to ascend as quietly as possible.

Then, enlarging a weakness in the wall of the Chapel, he was able to access the Penthouse and progress from there onto the roof. The chimneys from the cells over the Ordinary's house must have enabled him to hang on and slowly traverse the roofs until he found an unoccupied house, once belonging to a pastry-cook, just beyond the confines of the prison.

He later described how he put his shoes back on and attempted to conceal his fetters by wrapping them around with rags and pieces of his coat. In that way, he was able to descend and exit into Phoenix Court and thence into the street, appearing to any observer in the darkness as if he were just a gouty old man staggering home. From there, encumbered by the weight of his chains he was nevertheless able to walk to his home in Nightingale Lane. He must have known a smith, for by the time guards arrived at his home, he was gone and the fetters were found cut through and abandoned in an alley nearby.

Chapter 19
The words of Clarence Germane ~ June 1736

When you are neighbour to thieves and cut-throats, it pays to be on good terms with them. As a man whose skills and trade are in constant demand, I have not found it overly necessary to blacken my reputation with felony and transgression. However, on occasion, it can be both profitable and even a mercy to apply my skills in ways that are not strictly legal. When two ladies I knew well came knocking at my door in the dead of night, I needed but a little persuasion to go to their aid. I refer of course to Dan Malden's intrepid escape from Newgate. Ah, what a night that was.

Malden's woman, the one they call Mudge was there along with Elizabeth Shelton. They were anxious I brought tools and came with them. Nightingale Lane is not far from my home, and that is where we were headed. It was a blustery night and the moon kept diving behind clouds and re-emerging. The old Tower was silhouetted against the moonlit as we reached the Maldens' lodgings.

I had been led to believe speed was of the essence, and the two ladies had been very secretive. I was intrigued and puzzled but I never in a thousand years expected to find Dan Malden there. He was in quite a state when I first saw him, exhausted; already weak from two months in gaol, desperate to rid himself of those dreadful chains. They must have weighed half a hundredweight, and as you know, he was not a big man. Still, I knew how to apply my tools to good effect and soon had him free, albeit a shade more bruised than he had been. Where the chains had cut into his flesh needed a great deal of attention, but that was for others to attend to. I took my leave and left them to it. I had no wish to be taken up for interference in the process of law so I hurried away home. I left them to dispose of the irons. I wanted no part of it. I told no-one of what I had done, not even my wife, Temperance, who was sleeping off a heavy bout of drinking the night before. I was not sure she would have approved.

She went out early the next day. I had not realised she intended to attend the hangings. She came back with a story to tell.

"Do you know," she said, "they only hanged four instead of five. The crowd was right disappointed."

"Did someone get a reprieve?" I asked, pretending I knew less than I did.

"Well, that's the thing," she continued. "That Dan Malden - he's escaped. The watch are searching his home and all the public houses and taverns he frequents, but no-one has seen hide nor hair of him. He's vanished, and still all bound in chains, they do say." She then looked at me in a strange way, and for a moment I wondered if she had guessed, but I held my expression and she relaxed. As soon as she had averted her gaze, I heaved a sigh of relief.

Then I heard the full story of his escape. All I can say is it is a good thing he was small. That little fellow could wriggle through gaps that those of us who boast a fuller figure could never entertain.

Over the subsequent days, there were so many stories banded around suggesting where that young ruffian might be found. A reward was posted offering twenty guineas to anyone that might have information leading to his apprehension. I was worried for him. There were those who called themselves his friends who would have sold their whole families for a sum like that.

On Thursday of that week, after Malden had been at large for the best part of four days, a boy called at my forge with a message. It was most crudely written and I found it hard to decipher, but the words of the messenger were enough to make me stop what I was doing and travel west in search of its writer.

"Who gave you this message to deliver, boy?" I asked.

"A gen'leman, sir, a small gen'leman not much taller than me, sir."

"And where might I find this gentleman of whom you speak?" I asked him.

"He was most particular I only give that information to a smith called Clarence Germane, sir."

"And are you satisfied that is who you have found?"

"Sir?"

"Am I Clarence Germane, boy?"

"I hope so, sir," he whimpered."

I took pity on him.

"You are wise to be cautious. And you have indeed succeeded in discovering Clarence Germane. Now where am I to find the writer of this letter? If I am to come to him, I must know where he is."

That was when I learned that for the past four days he had been hiding well away from the places the authorities had been searching, at the sign of the Blackboy at Millbank, the house of a Mrs. Newman. The boy was her son.

On my arrival I let the lady know I had arrived and was shown into a back room. Daniel Malden looked a good deal better than the last time I had seen him. He was dressed in what can only be described as rags but at least he looked well enough in himself. Good food and a comfortable bed had restored him to some extent, but four days without company or activity had left him bored and in want of even the simplest diversion.

"It is so good to see you," he grinned as he clasped my hand in his. Mudge and Beth know where I am, but fear to come as they might be followed. I still prefer no-one else to know of my whereabouts. Added to that, I am afraid that there are those who will surmise that this is where I am as this was a house I once used to find customers for my girls. I used to meet here with Joseph Rose and my cousin on occasions. There must be those keen to get their hands on my bounty who might reasonably expect I might be here."

"So what do you want me to do?" I asked.

"Find me a place, just for a few days where I might safely be, where there is no connection between myself and the housekeeper. I did not know who to trust, but as you have already seen fit to help me in my plight, I assume you understand the meaning of a confidence."

"Let me give this matter a little thought," I said. "I have no doubt I can find you a haven. I have customers that have good reason to hold a trust in me and I will find you a place. Do not venture out under any circumstance. Too many people would recognise you. Send the boy to me later today and I will give him the address you seek. I shall not expose the two of us to the danger of meeting here again. It appears the Newman boy can be relied upon. When he brings you the address, go straight to it under cover of darkness."

I already had an idea in my mind as to where to send him, but of course I had to make it right with the lady concerned. I can now reveal her to have been a Mrs. Franklin, whose house was in Rosemary Lane, above a shoemaker's shop, close to the Rag Fair, and not far from my own workshop in White's yard. Later that day, I was able to send word with the boy giving the address and how to reach it. I also sent a second-hand suit I had purchased as close to his size as I could guess. He was in no fit state to go anywhere dressed the way he was. It was the least I could do.

It worried me that Dan was clearly bored and frustrated by being forced to stay in hiding. As I recalled that had been the undoing of that other great escaper, Jack Sheppard. Newgate was now a stronger fortress than those times and I was certain if he was taken, there was no way Dan Malden could ever hope to escape again. I couldn't have been more wrong.

But, bored he was. Though this change of scene undoubtedly helped, within a day he was feeling as though he had just exchanged one prison for another. The noise of people heading for the Rag Fair must have been audible from his room and I later learned he had sent message to Mudge by way of the shoemaker downstairs. They had met amid the bustle of the fair, assuming there was a certain anonymity achieved by losing themselves in the crowds. But they were seen and recognised, and though they attempted to head for their own home, Daniel Malden was taken and brought back to Newgate Gaol, where this time he was held in greatest security in the condemned hold, stapled down to the floor and double chained to await his appointed date with the hangman.

Chapter 20

The words of Mr. Akerman, warder of Newgate Gaol
~ June 1736

Within bartering distance of the Rag Fair and just off Rosemary Lane is a certain gin shop, one of many such establishments which blight our good city. And it is there, I gather, that the man Malden was identified, together with that woman of his. Though, I am told, he attempted to take flight, he was subsequently apprehended and brought back to complete his sentence. By that, I mean his appointment with 'Jack Ketch' at Tyburn. He wouldn't want to disappoint his audience, now would he? He had unfinished business too with the Ordinary. The poor man hates to miss out on a good confession. He would hardly survive on what we pay him. No, it is the two hundred pounds or so a year he makes from selling confessions to the printers at Seven Dials that keep him in gin and oysters, which seem to form the staple part of his diet.

If I sound disapproving, I suppose I am. I believe in fitness of body and mind. It is hard to manage the affairs of others when your own constitution is weakened by an over-reliance on those substances known to be injurious to the soul. So many of those passing through my hands, in many cases those I employ as well as their charges, with more temperance might have made more of their lives. Like the man Malden - recaptured because he couldn't forego a cup of gin and a pair of welcoming thighs.

When he came back that time, he had a grin on his face - I swear it - and he just said, over and over, "Maybe now they'll remember me."

I just humoured him.

"I'm sure they will," I replied, though who he meant by 'they' I have no idea.

Escapes from Newgate are more common than you might

imagine, though most prisoners, if they survive the attempt, are recaptured within a few hours. It is difficult to make a totally secure prison. There are too many walls, too many ways in and out. The determined criminal will always find a way to break free. They will saw through metal, break brick and sever stone to save their miserable necks.

Escapes are an irritation. They generate additional paper work; further court appearances. No sooner did we have Daniel Malden ensconced in the condemned cell than it was necessary to bring him back to the court of the King's Bench to apply for a further rule of execution. Now how inconvenient is that? More delay for the hangman! More opportunity for the purposeful and tenacious man to plan to break free.

Still, few ever flee the condemned cell. It is a most strong and secure place, built under the house that might have been my own, had I chosen to live there. It is enough to suffer the squalid conditions of Newgate without having to spend one's whole life there. Then, one would be every bit as much of a prisoner as the worst felon.

Memories were still fresh of the escapes of Jack Sheppard, and it would have been unthinkable that Daniel Malden should be permitted to free himself again. On this occasion I appointed the man Isaac Austin to watch over Malden most carefully, when not attending to his other charges.

It is an odd thing, and not well remembered, but four men had attempted to make their escape from that cell ten years ago, by finding their way into the sewers that run beneath the prison. One was recaptured and one remained at large. The other two were never accounted for and were believed lost in the attempt. I mention this as it has some bearing on the story I can now relate.

On the evening of Sunday June 13th, I spoke to Austen about Malden and the other man condemned, one George Watson. Watson was a nasty piece of humanity, a murderer of the vilest kind. He was a violent and difficult prisoner and was held, for his sins, in the press room right opposite Jack Ketch's kitchen so he could suffer the pain of looking daily upon the man responsible for managing the machine of his death, when the appointed time came.

Austen's house was directly above the condemned hold, just inside the prison gate. As I have indicated, I choose to dwell outside the confines of the gaol. I had just returned from evening service at my chosen place of worship, when I was accosted by Mr. Austen

"I am concerned," he informed me, "that the man Watson may attempt to put an end to himself." This was not unknown. Even the notorious Jonathan Wilde had swallowed poison before his execution. It had not brought about his end, but it had rendered him insensible to the punishment he so richly deserved. In the end, our man Thrift had to lift him bodily to put the noose around his neck. It was not what the crowd wanted and they pelted him as he hung. Another, I remember, who was more successful in cheating the hangman was dragged to a crossroad and there buried with a stake driven through his heart.

We looked in at Malden. He seemed quiet, settled and well secured. I was confident he would not find these walls so easy to breach.

"We will attend to the man Watson," I said, and we left Dan Malden. He was chained to a staple driven into the floor. The irons alone must have weighed a hundredweight. His woman had been to see him earlier in the day. She had brought food and even a change of clothes for her man. She was popular with the warders as she tended to bring them little presents and make light of her man's situation.

Others would weep and plead, knowing what awaited their loved ones. It was odd, but she, like him, seemed resigned, almost accepting of his fate.

Newgate is a busy place by day. Those who can afford to pay can have anything they want there. All kinds of food and vittles, including the strongest liquors are brought in and as long as the warders are 'compensated' for their 'tolerance' it is seen as acceptable. Whores can be had by arrangement and all manner of other indulgences besides. I am not totally in favour of such things, but it is the way in which things have been managed for centuries and far be it from me to bring about unnecessary change. Satisfied prisoners give you less trouble, and the gratuities earned augment the meagre salaries paid to their keepers.

I spoke to Austin, recommending he use the utmost vigilance where Watson was concerned.

"Under no circumstances permit that man to deprive John Thrift of his fee," I said. "Even if it means we remain awake all night. I think I should look in on young Malden just once more, though I expect no trouble from him."

That Sunday night, it was quiet, by Newgate standards. The groans and the retching of the sick, the clanking of chains and voices in the street outside were all I remember as we attended to our duties - and most of our attention was focused on the need to keep a man alive so that he might be done to death in the morn... all part of the job... all part of the job.

Chapter 21
The words of Dan Malden ~ Whitsunday 1736 and after

The lanes and alleys of London are a mystery even to those who live there. They join prosperous streets to the meanest of yards; they offer throughways to nowhere that anyone would wish to go; they link the lives of the desperate to those who need fear nothing. And below those are other kinds of roadways. To enter the world of the sewers of London is not an undertaking to be entertained lightly. Worse than the smell and the dark and the rats are the other dangers - suffocation from the noxious fumes that build up in pockets underground, becoming lost in the maze that is that awful world, being stuck tight in the narrowest of channels or being drowned when the holes fill up following a deluge above. Yet it was that way I chose to make my second escape from Newgate prison.

John Holburt had put the idea in my mind. It had been done before, though others had died in the attempt. Such thoughts had been whispered to me during a visit to my cell. As John pointed out, one as slight as myself, but strong, had the best of chances, even though they had to be slim. He also said one thing that stuck in my mind...

"Don't forget, water runs downhill. If you get into the sewers, follow it down and you will come to the river."

Holburt came but the once. It was good of him, as he was at the time on bail awaiting trial for our attack on MacNeal. Though his plan for me had some appeal there was still the small question of separating my fetters and chains; no mean task. Mudge came each day with food and I welcomed her company. She got on well with the keepers. They trusted her to ease my final days. In this way, it was possible to be as close as you can get in a condemned cell. At times, we were left alone and given all the privacy we desired.

On the afternoon of the Sunday, she came for the second time that day. I was not expecting her. She brought with her three things, a knife, a piece of steel and a tinder-box. It was not difficult for her to pass these objects unseen so I could secrete them under my clothes.

The man Austen came to look in on me at about eight o'clock. I remember it being around the time the chimes from Christ Church rang out. He brought me a penny leaf to smoke and a bottle of small beer.

"These will help make these hours a little easier," he said. He also handed me a bottle of clean water. It was a kindness I shall remember him for and clearly marked the end of his attentions regarding myself for the night. If ever I was to escape, it had to be then, before the hours of daylight.

I waited until he had gone upstairs. It was extremely dark in the condemned cell, yet I knew every inch of it and everything that was in it. My hands closed around the steel that Mudge had brought me. It had a serrated edge. I felt for the chains that held me there. Though I would have liked to have freed myself closer to my body, that would have necessitated sawing through each chain in turn. No, given the time I had, it had to be the staple that held all my chains to the floor. It was roughly driven in, not properly forged, and though it meant escaping with two sets of chains still attached to me, it was the best of chances on offer.

I worked through that staple with much difficulty, but I was determined, and slowly it began to come loose. Then I heard a sound as of a warder returning. I moved a little so that whoever he was might find a reason for the sounds I had been making only moments before. It was Akerman, the chief keeper. I turned over as if trying to sleep. I heard his steps retreat, I hoped for the last time that night.

Little more was required to free the staple entirely, though I was very much aware of what an encumbrance my chains would be. Their weight and bulk was every bit the handicap they were intended to be, but it couldn't be helped. I set about making an escape from the cell. In the corner of the room, dark though it was, I knew there was a stone seat. I had already loosened it somewhat, so I knew there to be a row of iron bars just beneath it. Those bars were not put there for no reason. Their very presence made it clear to me there must be a passage beneath them.

Using my knife, I got the stone down and began to dig a passage under the bars. The only tools I had were my knife and the serrated iron, but I dug at the floor with a will. I was desperate. My nails were torn off the ends of my fingers and my hands were in a miserable condition by the time I had opened up a space just large enough for one small as myself to squeeze through. I pulled a blanket from my bed after me, and once through the gap, wrapped it around my waist. It was a wise decision.

I went in head foremost, but one of my legs, my irons being on, stuck fast in the hole, and by this leg I hung in the inside of the vault with my head downward for half an hour or more. I thought to myself, "I shall be stifled in this sad position and found dead by morning." I contemplated calling out, but thought of what I had achieved so far and determined I would by some means release myself.

It is odd, but in making such an escape, you value every inch toward freedom you have gained. Because of that, I was reluctant to make any movement back in the direction I had come from. Still, half an hour dangling in a hole gives you time to reconsider your plans, and it was by turning myself in the hole and reaching up, I was able to grasp one of the bars above and turn my body around.

I hung by one hand, using the other to free my chains, which dropped down beneath me. I knew I could not hang there for long like that. The immense weight of the chains was dragging me down. I had no idea of the depth I was to fall if I let go.

I had the idea that perhaps I could use the blanket in some way to lower myself gently down, but in attempting to tie it, I fell some distance and with much violence into a hole under the vault. The weigh of my irons drew me down with great force and I landed on them, bruising my flesh and winding myself to such an extent that I lay there for some time. I could no longer hear noises from the street and felt entirely alone in the blackness.

It was this that prompted me to use the flint and steel and tinder to make a light. The tinder was damp and only after warming it a while under my arm could it be coaxed into making a light. I had a small portion of pipe and made use of Austen's penny leaf as I contemplated my next move. Such light as I could conjure, showed my hole to be a funnel, very straight and narrowing down. Without my irons, I would have made this with ease, but encumbered by them, I found myself again stuck fast. I began to panic, pulling, squeezing, tearing the flesh off my bones in the attempt to free myself. Again, it was only when I stopped to think that I made progress. This narrow channel opened into the main sewer and here I knew lay the way to freedom. Pulling myself back, I fed my chains through the hole first, and it was the very weight of these in the end that pulled my exhausted body through.

Sitting in the commodious space, I now found myself beside an underground stream. I sought to wash the filth from my body and clothes. My shirt and breeches were torn in pieces and covered in all manner of foulness. I was unsure as to the nature of the murky waters that flowed through that underground channel, but it seemed a good deal cleaner than what I was already covered in. So I washed out my overclothes. For the first time that night I felt cold. It had been comfortably warm in my cell, but now in spite of all my exertions I found I was shivering and needed to move myself around to warm my body.

Now a new danger overtook me. I could distinctly hear voices. My escape had been discovered and several of the Newgate runners had been put into the sewer to look for me. Almost in despair, I pulled myself into a hollow place in the side of the brickwork, wrapping my clothes around my chains so they would not make a noise.

Three or four men passed within a foot or two of me, as I tried to quiet my heartbeat so they should not hear it as loud as I believed I could.

"He must have come this way," said one.

"More likely he's still stuck in the hole above or gone the wrong way entirely."

"No-one ever gets out of these sewers alive."

"That won't help us if he fails to make his appointment with the hangman."

"Oh my God!" called one. Now what?

"What is it? Oh, b'luddy hell!"

"You know what these are, don't you?"

I sat in that nook, listening to their conversation, with no idea what they had found. I only later discovered that others had tried to escape the way I had come, ten years earlier, only to be overcome by the fumes. My pursuers had found their remains - two sets of bones picked clean by the rats.

"The air must be foul here. We had better not stay."
I heard this parting remark and felt the same way myself, though I knew whatever the risk I could not yet move for fear of being discovered. I knew also that they would be back when they failed to find me further down, so there I stayed, even dozed a little, curled in a corner, reluctant to sleep in case I never woke up again.

I came to as I heard them returning. They moved on past, anxious to be out of the place, certain I would never leave there alive. As I heard their footsteps disappear, I wasn't sure they wouldn't prove to be correct.

Call it mawkish curiosity if you like, but the first thing I did as I pulled myself out of that hole was to make a light and look upon those whose earlier attempt at freedom had been so ill-fated. Somehow the fear of not looking at them was worse than the sight of their gritted teeth and the teeth marks on what remained of their ribs. I knew I would soon be free.

In actual fact, it took longer than I would ever have imagined. Though I remembered Holburt's advice, passages separated, water lay in stagnant pools and it was a full thirty-six hours before I came upon a means of exit, not a thousand miles from where I had started. I encountered a machine; a device which afforded a means of making my way out of those sewers alive, just as I was almost devoid of hope. It was a pump, located in the Town Ditch, I discovered, at the rear of the school known as Christ's Hospital. It sat at one end of a yard. A woman was washing some clothes and seeing me emerging in the state I was, chains trailing behind me, was all for raising the alarm.

But she was a simple soul and it was easy to deceive her.

"I have been dragging these chains to clear the sewer. Now I must away to the smith to have them unattached."

She looked bemused, but was prepared to accept such an explanation. But it made me aware of the need to cover my chains if I was to make my way to safety. I tore my west-coat into strips wide enough to conceal the chains, though they made my legs appear mighty huge. I was weak from hunger and the weight of the irons was even more of a handicap than hitherto.

As luck would have it, a friend from the past spotted me. With a hint of recognition, a man I had once known in our days of managing the girls happened to be driving past in a rude kind of a carriage. I suppose it was little better than a porter's cart but it would take me back to White's Yard, where I knew I could find all the things I needed.

First stop was Clarence Germane's workshop where I assumed I would be able to rid myself of my chains, but the man was having none of it this time. The Newgate people had been there already and Germane wanted me away before he could be accused of aiding and abetting my escape. They were sure he had helped me the previous time. Now they had filled his head with the fear of what he might suffer should he remove my chains again.

Once again, Elizabeth Shelton was my saviour. She swore at Germane. "Of all we have done in the name of friendship for you!"

"I shall still not grind off his fetters this time - not even for a hundred pounds!" shouted the smith. I have sworn I have not seen this man and that I would not be any part in his escape this time. Would you have me swear to a lie?"

"Yes, I would, in the name of friendship!"

"Then give me the use of your tools and I shall do it," she yelled. And I think she would have done, except another neighbour, one Richard Cooper, who had done work with Germane took on the task. There were a great many chains and knocking apart the rivets holding them was no easy task. Applying heat was out of the question. Heat one link and the rest of the chain becomes so unbearably hot the pain is impossible to suffer. In the end, it was the skilful application of tools and a proper use of force that took away my irons.

I received food, a good washing and new clothes were sent for. Mudge appeared. They had been to question her about my escape and she was fearful she would lead them back to me again. It was reasonably suggested it would be unwise for me to remain in the Yard so Beth Shelton, bless her, arranged for me to rest up a few days with a woman she knew, close to the Ratcliffe Highway.

Then, it was planned I should make for Harwich and go across the water to Flushing, maybe even taking service with His Majesty's Navy again. One thing was certain; I could not remain in London. So, still unsure this was what I really wanted, I went with friends to Enfield where a suit was purchased for me and I was put aboard a coach for the Essex coast.

Chapter 22
The words of Richard Turpin: alias, John Palmer
~ August 1736

Nobody was supposed to know I was there, or even the name by which I was then attempting to pass myself, so imagine my surprise and horror when my landlord appears with the most unexpected of comments: "A visitor to see you, Mr. Palmer... goes by the name of Mr. Morgan."

I did not know whether to prime my gun or leap of out the window, but I was curious to discover just who this Morgan character might be.

"Good Lord!" I ejaculated, because, to my surprise, I recognised him. I had only met Dan Malden two or three times before. It seemed unlikely our paths would cross again. Not a lot of people find their way to the fenlands around Lincoln. That was what appealed to me about the area. But here, the two most wanted felons in England were shaking hands and engaged in conversation together. It would have appeared a bizarre scene. He was unaccompanied so far as I could see. He looked a little older and more battle-scarred. He had lost his front teeth for a start, but he still looked little more than a child, and had a green jockey's cap on his head as if to advertise to all the world that this was who he was.

It seemed, my secret hideaway was not quite secret enough. I was, for all that, quite pleased to see him. It was late Summer in 1736 and all my colleagues were gone. The three Gregory boys were dead, one from a gunshot wound, the other two hanged and gibbeted. Fielder, Rose, Haines and Saunders had met the same end. Humphrey Walker had died in prison. Mary Brazier was bound for in slavery in America and John Jones awaited a similar fate. Tom Rowden had just been arrested. It seemed I was the only one left.

"I had heard you had gone to the Low Countries," Malden said.

"I still intend to," I told him. That was the rumour I was aiming to cultivate. He needn't know I had no intention of crossing any stretch of water wider than the Humber.

"I may take that route myself," he said. "I have served the King before. I may sign aboard a naval vessel."

"Who knows you are here?" I asked.

"If you are more concerned who knows *you* are here, then rest assured, your secret is safe with Country Jack."

But I knew my secret was not safe. It would never be safe whilst one man may save his own neck by offering himself as an evidence against another. It was then I knew I must move further north, telling nobody of my plans.

"Go then," I told him, "and tell the world that Turpin is gone abroad, and I shall say the same of you if that is what you would have me say."

Because, at the end of the day, we both knew our hearts lay here, in England and whatever dangers that might cause to prevail, this was where we were really intending to stay.

We took a jug of ale together and talked about old times. I learned he had intended to go overseas, but had changed his mind on meeting up again with Country Jack. Confound the man, he made it his business to know where everyone was! I gather it wasn't a chance meeting. Young Malden had been once before with Jack to a village south of Chelmsford. Playing a hunch that that was where he might find him, he had abandoned his intention of finding a ship and had ridden there.

"So what turned you away from quitting these shores?" I asked him.

"A chance encounter in a Harwich hostelry with a sailor," he told me.

Word had been sent post-haste to all ports to watch for the gaol-breaker, Daniel Malden. It was the news of the day and spoken of everywhere in the town. That innocent face was what saved him that time. It never occurred to the sailor in question that one so infant-faced could be a notorious felon. Dan had turned around and made his way inland. Finding Country Jack, he had borrowed enough to keep him a week or two and extracted the intelligence as to where I might be found.

Dan Malden never made it clear why he had sought me out. I suspect he was hopeful I was still riding the roads and thought he could team up with me. But I could see my days of that pursuit were over. Too many young men had taken a fancy to the reward on my head and too many companies of foot were under orders to shoot me on sight.

However, it was easy to believe I was still as active as ever. hardly a day went by without a newspaper story somewhere being published that I had committed some fresh outrage. It seemed I was responsible for every highway robbery from Exeter to York. All that in spite of the fact I had never stayed so honest for so long in my life before.

"Perhaps," he called out as he rode away, "we shall meet again in Antwerp."

That was the last time either of us saw the other, but I can tell you one thing, I later that month read reports in a number of newspapers describing how both Turpin the butcher and Dan Malden the gaol-breaker had taken themselves across the sea to Holland and were not intending to return.

Chapter 23
The words of Mary Malden, otherwise known as Mudge ~ September 1736

"I've sat and waited for you. I've been at your beck and call. I have lived in some of the least pleasant places on the face of God's earth. I have even lied for you. Now I want to go home. Is that so unreasonable?"

To be honest, I had drunk a fair bit that afternoon, but I was also seething with discontent. I had helped spread the word that he had joined service against the King's enemies. It was anyone's guess what he had really been up to. He owed a number of our friends a good deal of money, yet when I finally caught up with him, he was prosperously kitted out, and spending money like water.

"I've heard nothing from you for a month or more," he complained.

"Are you surprised? How many times have the Newgate runners been to Rag Fair asking their questions?"

It was true, they had trailed around after anybody that had known Dan Malden in the hope of finding him again. So often criminals cannot relinquish their favourite haunts. Well, they may have been his favourite haunts, but they weren't mine. At the first hint that Dan had settled somewhere different, I was off and I just hoped that my departure had gone unnoticed.

It was a warm September day in a stable boys' beer house close to the Canterbury racecourse, and this was no more where I wanted to be than White's Yard.

"*You* look grand enough; *I* look like a fish wife. Give me some of the money you obviously have and I can be dressed as finely as you."

"My costume is going to earn me some money."

I did not understand.

"I have ridden horses here before," he said. "If I look the part, I will *be* the part, so to speak."

So there it was, the old ambition to ride horses. If that was the plan, why was he under sentence of death for stealing a miserable pile of someone else's washing?

He looked every inch the prosperous young man about the racecourse. He had a plate-buttoned coat, a silk waistcoat and breeches and a velvet riding cap.

Dan had left London in something of a hurry. He had travelled north and claimed he had even met Turpin, before boarding a ship at Hull. I think even then he had intended to go to Holland, but the ship took in crew and supplies at Chatham, and realising how close to Canterbury he was, Dan had made for one of our old haunts and picked up a few rides. Once settled, he had sent for me, and like the faithful little wife (if wife I ever was), I followed him South. But as so often in our relationship, it was not to be all plain sailing.

It had been a terrible summer in our part of London. At the beginning of August, trouble had broken out between the labouring Irishmen, who were plentiful in the area, and the English. The Irish were prepared to work for wages, most of us would have spurned even if we had been starving. Some of them made much of the fact they could lift more, dig more and carry more than their English counterparts. Fuelled by drink, what had started as a public house brawl spilled out into the streets of Spitalfields, Shoreditch and Rosemary Lane, where battle commenced. A lad was shot in the Minories, and for a while rioters from both sides ruled the streets. Gradually, as Companies of Foot and of Horse were sent in, law and order prevailed, but it was an uneasy peace and we had been virtually house-bound at night and ever in fear of house-breakers and fire-raisers driving us out to the mercy of the mob.

I was resentful about being left alone to cope with weeks of disorder whilst he had apparently been out enjoying himself. As I said, I'd had a good bit to drink and I was altogether too loud and altogether incautious.

"So I am dependent on your generosity for what little I get, which right now appears to be nothing!"

"Oh just wait a day or two while I attract the right sort of rides."

"You're sure you haven't got some other irons in the fire?" I continued. With all this horsemanship, maybe you can pick up where your good friend Turpin has left off - relieving travellers of their valuables along the Pilgrims Way."

I was loud - dangerously loud and I should have known better, but the drink was in me and the sense was not. I should have known someone would hear and start to ask questions.

"Perhaps, as you already have an appointment with Jack Ketch, you would like to widen your experience. Why not steal from churches, from judges, from kings - why, there is no limit when you are already condemned. After all, you can hang just the same for stealing a whole flock of sheep as for one lamb."

We went on like this at some length. I really can't remember all the accusations that were thrown to and fro, or just how noisily they were delivered.

Perhaps there was a shuffling in the room next door; perhaps it was all my imagination. It's hard to remember. Dan barely seemed to have noticed.

"I'll have you know: all this, (he waved his fancy cuffs at me) I came by honestly. For once, I don't need to steal. People round here value what I can do. And if you weren't such a stupid bitch, you'd see it!"

Then, a lot of things happened at once. Two constables and the local watchman burst in. We were both taken and questioned. I said nothing. I sobered up very quickly at the shock of it all, and I knew it was better if they did not know who it was they had arrested. We were spoken to in different rooms. This did not help our cause. I gave my name as Morgan; Dan said he was Smith. We both claimed to be married.

The lad that had reported us had been supping in the next

room when he heard us arguing. Thinking from what of our conversation he could hear that he might have detected a famous highwayman, he had run along to the authorities, in the hope there might be a reward payable on arrest.

Whether he ever received any reward is unlikely. Very rarely did such payouts go to those who believed they had earned them. What was clear was Dan was in serious trouble. Mention of his being a condemned man had aroused interest. They knew he had not been sentenced in Kent, so word was sent to London for descriptions of any prisoners at liberty.

Dan was ever the easy one to recognise. He was small, had two missing front teeth, even a small inked picture on his arm from when he was a sailor. One of the keepers at Newgate drew sketches of those capitally convicted. Within a day or two the warders at Canterbury Prison had no doubt who they held in their most secure cell. One of the servants that had attended to Dan in Newgate, Abraham Mendez, came down to Canterbury to make the positive identification.

I tried to see Dan but to begin with he refused to have anything to do with me. I was close enough to hear him shout, "I have no desire to see the damned bitch that betrayed me!" I could not have felt worse.

But after a day or two of trying, I was shown to his cell. It was every bit as gloomy and depressing as the condemned cell at Newgate. Having discovered he really was Malden the gaol-breaker, they had chained him to several stapled points on the ground. They were taking no chances.

"You know they are sending half a regiment to bring me back," he laughed. He seemed almost proud. I wanted to cry. Though we were at all points overlooked, he held me close and whispered into my ear. "I have a plan. Listen."

That was how we came to be in church in Canterbury the following day. After I had left him that day, they had sent a priest to try to extract a confession from him. Daniel, ever the actor, had come on all penitent and bitterly regretting his past transgressions.

He had pleaded to go to church, to make his peace with God. The priest, believing in the power of his appeals to Dan agreed - even wrote a sermon designed to bring him closer to the Lord. It was widely published within hours that this special service would be held, and so it was I turned up to see Dan surrounded by warders being escorted to church, where a special sermon had been penned on his behalf..

He certainly seemed sorry. He wept profusely and re quested that I should be permitted to sit with him. His cries were of a concern to the parson, so, seeing he was still well-chained, I was permitted to comfort him. At length, he calmed a good deal and the minister was able to offer his advice to 'the man about to leave this world.'

As I clung to him, I passed a number of tools to Daniel - anything I had surreptitiously been able to obtain that seemed useful in what I hoped might be his third escape - a malnspike, such as is used by basket maskers, a compass-saw for sawing boards, a piece of a sword that had been made jagged to cut iron, a knife and a large nail. Nobody appeared to notice.

At the end of the service, I thanked the parson and went my own way, still believing Dan would escape again. But it was not to be. He had indeed loosened some of the floor planking and had attempted to saw through a chain link when they discovered all the tools he had secreted about his person.

Later that day, Akerman arrived from Newgate. He was a renowned athlete and had run fom London to Canterbury.

An armed escort of thirty or forty horsemen soon followed. I saw them leave. Dan was taken on horseback with his legs chained under the horse's belly. Crowds lined the streets to see him go. I read later that similar numbers thronged the roadsides all the way to London, such was his notoriety. They spoke of him in the same breath as the great Jack Sheppard.

It took me a little longer to return to London. It was much harder to visit him now. People who had never met him queued to see him chained into an iron chair stapled to the floor. He was guarded day and night. When I did get to see him, you know what he said?

"They're going to remember me now." That seemed to please him. He remained hopeful that, as he had worked honestly since his escape and done no robbery, he might see his sentence altered to one of transportation for life. But it wasn't to be: like so many of his kind Dan Malden was to end his short life at the end of a rope. He was just twenty-three years old.

And so it was, along with two highway robbers, Dan Malden finally made the journey down Holborn to the gallows at Tyburn. The Ordinary said much by way of prayers, and we saw Dan brought out and put into the cart.

I say, 'we.' There were three of us there, though I know other friends saw him along the way that day. Beth Shelton was there at the prison lodge, as was Dan's father. It must have been hardest for him. He told the rest of the family to stay home. He bore his suffering on behalf of the whole family. Dan saw us as he came out and cried aloud that we should pray for him. Then he pulled off that awful old green jockey cap he used to wear and threw it to his father.

The mob behaved the way the mob usually did, I am afraid, with dirt and rotten fruit and vegetables and their coarse and vulgar hanging songs. The priest's prayers were drowned out by shouts and shrieks and cat-calls. All three executed that day did much as could be expected of them: appealed to the crowd to... "take warning at this our just and appropriate punishment." They then left the stage, crying out such words as, "God have mercy on my soul!" and "Lord Jesus receive my spirit." It might have been moving if one of them had not have been the only man I ever really loved.

It is an odd thing, but I found I could not look away, even after his last movements ceased several minutes later, I still looked at him and in that limp puppet-like corpse, could still see the same young boy I had first met all that time ago.

I heard that a surgeon had paid six pounds and twelve shillings for the right to anatomise his body. The doctor's handiwork was on display in the hall of the medical school. I did not attend. I stayed just long enough to go with his father to collect his remains and we took them back with us to Ipswich. Unable to give him a real Christian burial, we buried him by the foreshore where old Tom Brasier still exercises the horses. We interred his green jockey's cap with him.

The fine clothes he was wearing when he was arrested were never returned. I suppose they sold them. They sold copies of his last confession, but interest soon waned and you could find them only days later, fluttering on the wind, blown across the streets of London.

Strangely, pamphlets relating the escapes of Daniel Malden have continued to be published, not only in the town where he was born, but across the country. And every time someone escapes from gaol anywhere, they talk of them 'doing a Daniel Malden.' So, you see, his name has been remembered. He would have liked that.

Notes

Whilst this is a far from exhaustive list of references used in researching Daniel Malden's story, it should help to demonstrate how this tale has come to be written.

One of the earliest references is a rare book by James Caulfield entitled 'Portraits, Memoirs and Characters of Remarkable Persons from the Revolution in 1688 to the end of the Reign of George II, Collected from the most Authentic Accounts Extant.' (1819). Unfortunately certain details published here as fact are at odds with other contemporary information now available, and are almost certainly wrong. Investigations into other biographies in Caulfield's book show it to be no more reliable. The problem is compounded by the fact other sources such as the Oxford Dictionary of National Biography have used this and reitterated the same mistakes. For all that, both are useful to an extent and I believe I have sorted 'the corn from the chaff.'

Chapter 1

The words of Daniel Malden Senior ~ 1712   Page 7

From the parish registers of St. Matthews:
Daniel Malden [senior] married Mary Brasier Jan. 18th 1712. The baptisms of four of their children are there: Mary - Nov. 1713, Sarah - June 1717, John (Molding) - May 1721 & Elizabeth (Molding) - June 1727. There is no entry for Daniel. The Oxford Dictionary of National Biography suggests he may have been born in Canterbury, but most contemporary evidence shows he came from St. Matthews parish, Ipswich.
Early descriptions of Ipswich owe much to Daniel Defoe's 'Tour of the Eastern Counties' and 'Ipswich from the 1st to the 3rd Millennium' - Ipswich Society. The story of the midwife in the church porch is taken from an account in the Bury Post, Aug. 1797.
The cormorant and the eel episode, I observed recently from a boat at Orford. Several books detail Dr. Beeston's herb garden.
It may be just a coincidence that one of Dick Turpin's gang, Mary Brasier shares a name with Dan Malden's mother, but as is shown later, there are other connections between Malden and the Essex gang.
The smuggling details come mainly from newspaper accounts of the time, the writings of Alan Jobson & 'A Suffolk Coast Garland,' by Ernest Cooper (1928). Some of the best tales appear in my own books of early local newspaper stories.
Dockyard detail was added after reading: 'Ships & Shipyards of Ipswich' by Hugh Moffatt, 'Sprits & Lugsails' by John Leather and 'Once upon a Tide' by Hervey Benham, to mention a few.

Chapter 2
The words of Mary Malden ~ 1721 & 1723   Page 21

Horseracing detail comes from a host of references I found at Newmarket Racing Museum as well as several detailed accounts in copies of the Ipswich Journal and Suffolk Mercury of the time. A particularly good one is in the Journal of May 2nd 1730.

Bluecoat foundation minute books and lists of admissions still survive at Ipswich Record office (GA400/1/6 and GA400/2/1) and include details of Daniel's brother John who was bound in 1735 to a house carpenter.

Daniel Malden's final confession (See notes for Chapter 23) suggests that his parents attempted to see him educated, "but being a perverse boy, he scarce minded anything either of learning or Christianity."

Chapter 3
The words of Hannah Morse ~ 1725   Page 32

Most important in the writing of this chapter was the Ipswich Borough Sessions Book 1721-1742 (ref: C/2/9/1/1/8/9) where on May 8th 1725, Hannah Moss was allowed £10 to prosecute Daniel Malden and full details of his trial appear {pages 88 - 89 in a form of Latin}. The jury names etc. come from this account.

Much later, in his obituary in an Ipswich Gazette of November 1736, it relates that 'in his youth he confederated with other boys, and being taken for breaking the shop of Mrs Morse of Ipswich, was whipped at the cart's tail.'

Chapter 4
The words of Thomas Brasier ~ 1727   Page 37

Dan Malden's newspaper obituary aforementioned, and his final confession tell of his becoming a jockey and riding for 'people of note in station.' Successive entries in the Oxford Dictionary of National Biography state he trained as a postillion, but I can find no reliable evidence of this.

Shrubland Hall would have appeared much different from the way it does today. The former building was replaced the present mansion in the 1770s.

Chapter 5
The words of Dan Malden ~ 1728   Page 45

Again, racing details are borrowed from contemporary newspapers. The race from Six Mile Bottom to Newmarket and back appeared in a 1728 Ipswich Journal as did the race where a man could not 'draw the weight.'

The Bungay to Trowse race happened at least once (but in reverse) for a purse of 200 guineas. My description comes by reference to the earliest maps available, using a bit of imagination.

Several top horses of the time had the word 'dragon' in their names.

Chapter 6
The words of 'Mudge'
(later to be known as Mary Malden) ~ 1728 & 1729   Page 57

All the Ipswich pubs in this book appear in lists found in the papers of the Ipswich historian, John Glyde and 'Ipswich 200 years ago' by H. Chamberlain, which supplied much other detail too.

The story of the horrific punishment inflicted on an English sailor on a Low Country port was reported in Norfolk and Suffolk papers in August 1728 Browne, Green & Smith really were horse thieves, two of them hanging at Thetford (Norwich Gazette: April 1729)

The thunderstorm (page 66) was real, as was the reference to the four killed 20 years earlier. Newspapers at the time made a similar conection.

Chapter 7
The words of Dan Malden ~ 1729 & 1730   Page 69

Sailmaking - The classic reference is 'The Sailmaker's Apprentice' by Emiliano Marino (1994), which proved invaluable.

Though we have no record of Dan Malden's life at sea, both his final confession (see notes for chapter 23) and his entry in the Oxf. Dict. of Nat. Biog. quote his visiting Gibraltar and Portugal in the Mediterranean, and also his earlier apprenticeship to a sailmaker.

Accounts of life at sea come from a day spent in the library of the National Maritime Museum, and come from so many sources it would be impossible to list them all. One book was particularly useful - 'Jack tar - a sailor's life' by J. Welles Henderson & Rodney P. Carlisle.

Chapter 8
The words of Daniel Malden Senior ~ 1730   Page 77

Joseph Rose, mentioned often in this book, now as the lover of Mary Brasier, is given some mention in 'Dick Turpin - The myth of the English highwayman' by James Sharpe, as are others of the Essex gang, such as Thomas Rowden and the Gregory boys.

Chapter 9
The words of Midshipman Andrew Carter   Page 81
~ 1731 & 1732

References for this chapter are similar to those for chapter 7. Costume is contemporary as, I hope, is all other detail. Again we take the places to which Malden claimed to have travelled from his final confession. There seems no reason for this to be inaccurate.

A fine account of a sea rescue appears in the Ipswich Gazette, Jan. 10th 1736.

Chapter 10
The words of Joseph Rose ~ 1733   Page 88
Some of the detail relating to meeting places and 'safe houses' comes from the aforementioned book by James Sharpe about Dick Turpin.

Prostitution in the eighteenth century is well covered in 'The Covent Garden Ladies' by Hallie Rubenhold.

Names like George Scroggs (page 90) are taken from contemporary newspapers, as is the robbery of Mr. Venables at Sydenham, where an Irishman named Murphey, alias Bourke, did actually die, though his colleagues were never found. (Ipswich Gazette: Nov. 24th 1733)

Chapter 11
The words of Mudge   Page 98
(later to be known as Mary Malden) ~ 1733
Country Jack is a mysterious figure whose name crops up in a number of places, in particular regarding an Old Bailey case of 1736 where he and Daniel Malden were supposed to have aided Thomas George in the theft of a quart silver mug (see page 141). The robbery of MacGray appears in the Ipswich Gazette of Oct. 9th 1733, though the wounded highwayman was never identified.

Chapter 12
The words of Country Jack ~ Late 1733   Page 103
East London detail comes from a number of sources, especially 'London, Old and New', vols I and II by Walter Thornbury (1881) and the website: **www.mernick.co.uk/thhol**, the last five letters of which stand for 'Tower Hamlet history on line.' Old accounts of the area from a variety of sources can be found there, especially details of Well Close Square where we know the Maldens resided.

Executions for 'coining' appeared in the Suffolk Mercury and Ipswich Gazette. This particular one was reorted in the Gazette in December 1733.

Clarence and Temperance Germane, blacksmiths, were later mentioned in Old Bailey proceedings as neighbours of Daniel Malden.

Chapter 13
The words of John Holburt ~ Early 1734   Page 112
News reports from the Ipswich Gazette described unusually bad weather (Dec. 22nd 1733) and the employment of 100 men employed daily on terracing along the Thames at Kew (Feb. 14th 1734)

John Holburt appeared twice at the Old Bailey, associated with Dan Malden in cases of theft and was acquitted both times (Proceedings of the Old Bailey can be found online).

Press-gang activity was widely reported at the time, as was a clampdown on street-barrows (Ipswich Gazette: Feb 16th 1734, May 4th 1734)
King's birthday celebrations - Ipswich Gazette: Mar. 9th 1734. (This would be what we would describe as George II's official birthday - the anniversary of his accession to the throne). Royal Wedding - Ipswich Gazette: Mar. 23rd 1734.
The highwayman account on page 116 comes from the Gazette for March 16th 1734.
Further reading about London at the time can be found in 'Moll Flanders' by Daniel Defoe and the 'George Man' books by Keith Heller.

Chapter 14
The words of Country Jack ~ May 1734   page 118
I have chosen to put several reported robberies from the time down to these two. The ruined church is a Norfolk one I have transported in my mind to South Essex.
The fire at the inn in Gracechurch Street is reported in great detail in Ipswich Gazette: June 29th 1734.
Later news reports suggest Turpin and Malden met and discussed going to Holland (Ipswich Gazette: Sept. 1736). The suggestion is this was not their first meeting.

Chapter 15
The words of Mary Malden, otherwise to be known   Page 127
as Mudge ~ Summer 1734
Detail regarding Fleet marriages comes from 'London, Old and New' by Walter Thornbury (1881).
The MacNeal robbery actually happened in April 1735 and the trial of John Holburt came about over a year later in June 1736 after Dan Malden had been 'persuaded' to inform on his friend. (see Old Bailey Proceedings) Holburt was acquitted. I have chosen to set this crime about a year earlier.
Dan Malden's final confession includes the information that he had ridden horses at Canterbury after escaping gaol a second time. It is unlikely this was his first visit there. Caulfield's book makes his connection with Canterbury a stronger one, saying he was born and married there. This is most unlikely and I have no evidence he had ever been there before 1734.
The demise of the Essex gang is detailed in Sharpe's book about Dick Turpin, aforementioned. Of course, all this is in the newspapers of the time, as are the arrests of Thomas Winter (Ipswich Gazette: Sep 13th 1735) and Long Will Blackwell (Oct 4th 1735)
This newspaper also speaks of a kind of Martial Law being in operation at that time.

Chapter 16
The words of John Holburt ~ Winter 1735   Page 135
Weather reports: Ipswich Gazette: Jan. 24th & Feb. 28th 1736
The footpads trick was reported in the Gazette Oct 4th 1735, the pewter sign robbery: Oct 25th 1735, grave-robbers in April 1736.
The incident with Mudge becoming a highwaywoman is taken from a report appearing in the Ipswich Gazette on Nov. 29th 1735. All of these pieces had previously appeared in Bagnall's News, a London newspaper of the time.
The costume details regarding the 'Royal birthday' come from articles in the Ipswich Gazette dated Nov. 8th 1735 and May 1st 1736.

Chapter 17
The words of Dan Malden ~ February 1736   Page 141
The offence and trial involving Thomas George and Anne Evans is described in the Proceedings of the Old Bailey. Dan Malden and Country Jack are named and implicated but never charged. In Caulfield's book, this is described as the offence for which Dan Malden was finally hanged, clearly a mistake. However, it seems that the suggestion he was a bit of a specialist regarding stolen silver is most likely.
The robbery of Mary Henshaw by this gang is well described in the Old Bailey record of the trial. Reading the transcript, it is hard to understand how only Dan Malden was found guilty. Others seem to have been equally culpable. The transcript must be missing something. Other detail included here comes from Malden's final confession.

Chapter 18
The words of Isaac Austen (warder at Newgate)   Page 149
~ May 1736
The names of three Newgate keepers of the time find their way into surviving records. Austen (no Christian name given) comes in an Ipswich Gazette account of June 19th 1736. Abraham Mendez in Chapter 23 is the second.
Akerman, the head warder is mentioned in a number of places, including a book 'The Chronicles of Newgate' by A. Griffiths (1896) which includes a small picture of him. This book gives a lot of detail about Malden and his escapes but has the chronology wrong and cannot be wholly relied upon.
The names of those who hanged the day Malden escaped are listed online, as are all Tyburn executions of the time.
The Norwich Mercury for May 29th 1736 gives a detailed account of the manner of Dan Malden's first escape. Though the Caulfield book mentioned at the start of these notes speaks of Daniel Malden escaping with others, no newspaper accounts of the time agree with this.

Chapter 19
The words of Clarence Germane ~ June 1736   Page 152
In a trial of July 21st 1736, Elizabeth Shelton was tried at the Old Bailey for perverting justice in helping Daniel Malden after his escapes from gaol. Clarence and Temperance Germane are named as being present, and whilst Germane seems to have refused to remove Malden's chains the second time, it is inferred that he did so after the first escape. In the Old Bailey procedings of this trial, we learn of Malden's lost front teeth. Elizabeth Shelton was acquitted.

In the aforementioned 'Chronicles of Newgate' we have the Black Boy, Millbank, landlady Mrs. Newman, named as Malden's hideout.

The Ipswich Gazette and Norwich Mercury reported almost weekly on Malden's progress around this time as it became the story everyone wanted to read. His first recapture appears in the Gazette on June 5th, stating he was taken at a gin shop in Nightingale Lane by Rag Fair. This same paper gives us the real name of the Newgate hangman, John Thrift, commonly referred to, as all hangmen were, as Jack Ketch.

A later trial in 1738 of a Robert Hunt for theft in the Old Bailey proceedings names a bawdy house in Well Close Square as 'the place Daniel Malden was taken.' The landlady was named as Mrs. Bowers.

Chapter 20
The words of Mr. Akerman, warder of Newgate Gaol   Page 157
~ June 1736
We do know from Ipswich Gazette reports that Dan Malden was imprisoned the second time in the condemned cell. Plans in the 'Chronicles of Newgate' show this to have been under the keeper's house.

Akerman himself seems to have been widely respected and a very fit man as he is described by various sources as a 'renowned pedestrian.'

Chapter 21
The words of Dan Malden   Page 161
~ Whitsunday 1736 and after
There are conflicting reports of the second escape but it is well reported in the Ipswich Gazettes of June 19th & 26th 1736. The Caulfield book aforementioned, also the 'Chronicles of Newgate' and Malden's own confession to the Ordinary of Newgate (see notes to Chapter 23) add further colour.

Elizabeth Shelton's trial aforementioned details some of the help he must have enlisted.

George Watson, the other capital convict imprisoned there at the time was executed for murder at Tyburn on July 5th 1736

Chapter 22
The words of Richard Turpin: alias, John Palmer   Page 168
~ August 1736

One newspaper account has these two meeting - Ipswich Gazette: Sept. 24th 1736. It is even suggested they may have met in Holland. The Caulfield book says: 'a description of him was sent to every sea-port and public place in the kingdom.' As late as October 1735, the Ipswich Gazette had reported Turpin and Rowden riding openly and with impunity through the centre of London.

Turpin, still under the pseudonym, Palmer, was finally arrested, tried and hanged at York in 1739, having been living in the Humberside area for some time.

Chapter 23
The words of Mary Malden, otherwise known   Page 171
as Mudge ~ September 1736

Two rather different accounts of Malden's recapture and his wife's attempt to help him escape again appear in Ipswich Gazette Sept. 24th 1736 and Norwich Mercury Sept. 25th 1736, giving good descriptions of him.

The riots involving Irishmen in the East of London was the main news of the summer and constantly reported. The engraving on the title page of this book is by R. Grave and appears in the James Caulfield book mentioned earlier.

The £6 12s paid by a surgeon to anatomise him was Malden's own estimate, published in the Ipswich Gazette Sept. 24th 1736.

Further detail of Malden comes from the Gazettes of Oct. 8th and 22nd 1736.

Malden, in his final confession to the Ordinary, tried to show himself in the best possible light, claiming he had been condemned for his first offence and had been 'going straight' since escaping. (He hoped for a reprieve even though it would have meant transportation for life). It is unlikely either claim was true.

'The Ordinary' of Newgate was the Prison Chaplain whose duty it was to provide spiritual care to prisoners condemned to death. One of the perks of his job was the right to publish the prisoner's last confession together with an account of his life. This was a profitable sideline, earning him around £200 a year.

Following an execution and subsequent dissection by the surgeons, the family had the right to bury the remains, but not in consecrated ground. We have no idea where Daniel Malden's remains ended up, but according to reports of his execution, (Ipswich Gazette: November 4th 1736, The American Weekly Mercury of Philadelphia: March 24th 1737) friends or family were at the gaol door when he was brought out.

He was not forgotten. In 1764, the printers, Dicey and Marshall, in their catalogue of pamphlets included... 'The surprising escape of Daniel Malden out of Newgate, and true description of how it was performed two several times.'